NEVER SAY NEVER

I0623203

BRENDA BARRETT

JAMAICA
TREASURES

Never Say Never
A Jamaica Treasures Book/March 2017

Published by Jamaica Treasures
Kingston, Jamaica

978-976-8247-64-3
Jamaica Treasures
P.O. Box 482
Kingston 19
Jamaica W.I.
www.fiwibooks.com

ABOUT THE AUTHOR

Books have always been a big part of life for Jamaican born Brenda Barrett, she reports that she gets withdrawal symptoms if she does not consume at least two books per week. That is all she can manage these days, as her days are filled with writing, a natural progression from her love of reading. Currently, Brenda has several novels on the market, she writes predominantly in the historical fiction, Christian fiction, comedy and romance genres.

Apart from writing fictional books, Brenda writes for her blogs blackhair101.com; where she gives hair care tips and fiwibooks.com, where she shares about her writing life.

You can connect with Brenda online at:
Brenda-Barrett.com
Twitter.com/AuthorWriterBB
Facebook.com/AuthorBrendaBarrett

Prologue

Summer 2000

"Skyler Porter, is it?" Mrs. Beckett, the human resource director, looked over her glasses at Sky and then down at the resume in her hand before Sky could answer.

"You have an MBA from Harvard?" The lady looked up at her again. "How old are you?"

Sky resisted the urge to roll her eyes and point out that her age was at the top of the document.

"Twenty-two," she replied in a well-modified tone.

She needed this job—if she had to suffer through obvious questions, she would suffer through them. She had no idea why Jefferson Pharmaceuticals called her at the time they did even though she had not applied for the job. Nevertheless, it was an answer to prayers because she was at a crossroad in her life.

She had the option of staying in the States with her cousin, Addi, and find a job in New York, or return to Jamaica. The decision had been made for her with an invite to a job interview.

"How did you do it?" Mrs. Beckett leaned back in her chair.

"Do what?" Sky thought that she had missed something.

"Finished your undergraduate degree by twenty and your MBA by twenty-two?"

"I just worked hard," Sky said. "I did more courses than the usual in my undergraduate studies and graduated with a perfect GPA and then went to Harvard Business School on a scholarship."

Mrs. Beckett smiled. "I am impressed."

"Thank you." Sky nodded. She was now warming up to the stern looking woman.

"As you know this is a family-owned company. Travis Jefferson is the current president of this company. His father, Miguel Jefferson, started out selling cough syrup. Since the eighties, the business has grown exponentially.

"We are the leading pharmaceutical company in the Caribbean. We are a large company, and we continue to expand every day. This position of Business Development Manager is a senior management position, Miss Porter.

"Unfortunately, you have no experience whatsoever. You have a very nice degree, no doubt, but I am afraid that I can't in all good conscience recommend you for this position..."

Sky couldn't believe what she was hearing. She had not applied for this position. She had not even heard about it until she was asked to send in her resume. And now, after scraping together her airfare and spending her last dollar on an expensive suit, she was told this madness. Now, she would have to report the bad news to her father who had so exuberantly greeted her at the airport.

He had been excited at the possibilities of her living back home and closer to him. She was going to have to burst his bubble.

Sky got up slowly, disappointment ricocheting through her like fireworks.

Did this lady think that she had just been hanging out in Kingston? Did she have any idea how far she was coming from to be having this failed interview?

They could have done this over the phone!

"I am sorry Miss Porter." Mrs. Beckett held out her hand to be shaken.

She didn't look sorry.

Sky looked at her outstretched arm and for a split second considered being rude, but she didn't. She shook the lady's hand and searched for something to say that was pleasant, something that didn't scream her disappointment.

The door to the office was unceremoniously opened before she could formulate a word and a rather handsome guy pushed his head around the door.

"Oh good, she is here. Send her to my office Bertha, will you?"

Sky frowned and looked from Mrs. Beckett to the mysterious gentleman.

Mrs. Beckett looked miffed. "But I already checked her resume as you asked me to, sir, and I think..."

He came into the room fully. He was tall—over six feet. He had dark nutmeg brown skin and jet-black wavy hair, which was brushing his collar—some of it was falling in his chocolate brown eyes. He was the definition of tall, dark and handsome.

He pushed his hand into his suit pocket and looked at Sky for longer than was polite and then back at Mrs. Beckett.

"This interview was supposed to be a formality, Bertha. If I didn't have that meeting, I would have been around to welcome Sky into the Jefferson Pharmaceutical family."

And then his magnetic brown eyes were eating her up. "I am sorry for the misunderstanding, Skyler." He moved from the doorway and advanced to her with a smile in his eyes.

"My name is Travis Jefferson. Will you be so kind as to walk with me to my office?"

Sky nodded as if she was in a daze. He called her Sky with a hint of familiarity that was puzzling and exciting at the same time.

This was the Travis Jefferson, the head of the company. She had no idea he was so young, maybe early thirties and no idea that he was so attractive. Sky tried not to stare when she walked closer to him. She could smell his cologne— something earthy.

She had the insane urge to stop and sniff him. Instead, she concentrated on looking professional and followed him to the bank of elevators. His office was three floors up from where she met Mrs. Beckett.

He stood apart from her in the elevator and stared at her as if he wanted to say something.

Sky felt a bit self-conscious. She suffered through his silent regard and then followed him through the carpeted hallway and into his office.

Up here in the hallowed hallways of richness was obviously where the executives resided. Every door had a name embossed in brass, each of which had a VP of whatever on it.

His door was wider than the rest. There was a sub-office before another door. A lady who Sky assumed was his secretary was sitting at a desk. She was on the telephone.

"Hold my calls, Betty, and no visitors," Travis said before

they headed to another door, which Sky assumed was his office.

The office was large and tastefully done. One section of the wall was made of stone, with little niches in the wall, which were filled with flowerpots with bright looking plants—each blooming a different color.

A small conference table was at one end and in the middle was his desk. There was a patio filled with plants and a view of the mountains in the distance.

"Nice." Sky looked around. "This is a dream office."

Travis indicated for her to sit in a seat across from him and then he leaned over the desk smiling. "I have been keeping track of your educational pursuits, Miss Porter."

"You have?" Sky was trying not to act surprised.

But he could see that she was.

He scratched his head and then laughed. "My God, it's going to take time explaining this to you."

"What are you going on about?" Sky asked frowning. "Do you know me from somewhere?"

He smiled. "I believe I do, Miss Porter. Not from some other place but some other time."

Chapter One

"I can't believe I lost my books in the fire." Sky sat down heavily on the bed beside Addi. "My Econ texts could have gone up in flames for all I care, but my future book, the one that I had recorded the future prices of stocks and shares, is gone.

They had gotten the call last night from the security company that the hardware store was on fire.

This morning there was nothing left of the place. Where there once was a huge warehouse was now a big black hole of nothing.

Sky wished that she hadn't left her stuff there the night before. She had been working part-time at the store for the summer. Today was supposed to have been her last day.

Except there was no store.

It was a good thing she had handed in her Economics

assignments for the first summer session, or she would have been in deep trouble.

"I wish you had remembered that last night was the night of the fire, Addi," Sky said morosely. "Why didn't you write that down, record it for future reference, that would have been perfect!"

"I began losing the memories shortly after coming back. By the time, I thought to write down anything significant; I didn't know what was definite anymore. I am so sorry Sky. I did tell you about the fire in '95, didn't I?" Addi sighed. "I wish you hadn't taken your book to the store. Why did you take it there anyway?"

"I was copying the stuff to a new book." Sky felt a very real urge to cry. "I had stuff in there about '95.

"Now I am going to have to live my life like an ordinary person. Working summer jobs and applying for scholarships because I lost my future book with all my glorious future stock predictions. I had plans, Addi. I was going to be rich by twenty and retire by twenty-five."

"Hush," Addi said gently patting Sky on the shoulder. "It's not the end of the world. The good news is nobody was at the store when the fire started."

Sky sniffed and then stood up. She was going to mourn in her room in her empty, soulless house.

"Whatever Addison!"

"Wait!" Addi held on to her hand. "I have something to tell you. Now please, promise me that you will not explode."

Sky squinted her eyes and looked at Addi. They were both eighteen, but Addi was the calmer of the two. Sky was prone to volatile bursts of emotions. She was known to cry broken-heartedly, laugh loudly, and enact whatever she was feeling with gusto.

Addi was not so out there, with her feelings or reactions.

She had it all together. She was calm, mature and took things in stride. Maybe that was a leftover from her time traveling.

"No." Sky answered. Addi had always had it together since they were tots. She, on the other hand, was a volcano waiting to erupt.

"Well," Addi cleared her throat, obviously trying to choose carefully what to say.

"You know when you went to college last year, I applied to some colleges too?"

"Yes. So?" Sky knew she wasn't going to like where the conversation was going. She could see it from Addi's body language that she was expecting an overreaction from her.

"Well, Grandma Wallace filed for us. Mom and Dad said they wouldn't be leaving this year. Daddy said he is not sure he will ever be going. He doesn't want to leave Uncle Stan to run the business alone.

"Mommy said she is not leaving Daddy so..."

"So?" Sky wanted to squeal get on with it.

"So I guess I will be going alone," Addi said quickly, looking at Sky as if she expected retribution. "I have three college acceptance letters. I am thinking of taking the one to New York University."

Sky sat down on the bed again, feeling shell-shocked. "But this year you are supposed to join me at Mount Faith University!"

"I don't want to," Addi said stubbornly. "I am leaving, Sky. I think this is the best thing for me. I was thinking of doing psychology. I could live with Josh. He is in New York doing an internship at a tech firm."

Sky exhaled noisily. "But what about me? Have you thought about me? When you leave Jamaica, I'll have no one."

Addi covered a snort. "Sky, you have your dad and Monica

and your new baby brother, Michael."

"Good gosh, don't remind me about them," Sky muttered crossly. "Dad and Monica are caught up in a world of their own. If I disappeared now, they wouldn't care. Dad only cares about his new offspring—his long-awaited son."

Addi chuckled. "You love your baby brother."

"Well..." Sky's heart softened somewhat. He was a cute child. And sometimes she did think of him as the sweetest baby on the planet.

Her father and Monica Campbell from next door had started hitting it off almost as soon as the ink was dry on her parents' divorce papers. Two months after the divorce, they were married.

One year later they had a child together, and her father was acting like a first-time father.

It made her feel left out somehow. Monica was a lovely woman and quite accommodative, she had to admit grudgingly but Sky didn't feel comfortable in her house on the hill. Even after eighteen months she still thought of Monica as 'the lady next door', even when her father moved in with her.

Their home was not hers. After coming home from school, she spent most of her time with Addi anyway.

"And you have Aunt Ivy," Addi said haltingly because she knew that Sky did not have Ivy as a viable parenting option or even as a friend.

Sky glanced at her. "You know my mother is crazy. I can't have a regular conversation with her. Besides, any day now she will be going back to England to live."

"Well, there is always my mom and dad." Addi shrugged. "They are not leaving. They'll be right here. My mom is already talking about rebuilding."

"But they are not you," Sky said bitterly. "You deliberately and willfully want to leave me, Addison Porter. You are the worst cousin in the entire world."

Addison got up from the bed and stretched. "I am sure there are other cousins worst than I am."

Sky laid back on the bed and looked up at the ceiling. "I am not looking forward to going back to school in two weeks then. I was hoping you'd be there. Now my life sucks big time."

Addi chuckled and unraveled her hair from her messy top bun. "You'll be fine."

"No, I won't be fine." Sky turned on her back and hit the bed. "I won't be okay ever again."

Addi turned on the radio to drown out her tantrum.

"Hear this!" Addi pinched her. "This is your new jam, Waterfalls, TLC."

Sky grunted. "There is nothing, nothing at all that can make me happy again."

"So why are your feet moving up and down in tandem with the music?" Addi asked as she combed out her hair.

"It is a nice tune," Sky looked at Addi grudgingly. "This changes nothing. You are still the worst."

Addi didn't answer she just gave her a smirk and continued combing out her thick long hair.

Sky got up and stuck her face beside Addi's. They looked nothing alike except for the nose. They both had the Porter nose, short straight with a little flare at the end. That was where the similarities ended.

She wore cinnamon shade makeup for her lighter skin. Addi wore brown sugar for her darker complexion.

Sky had freckles on her nose bridge, little-discolored imperfections that increased with exposure to the sun. Addi's skin was smooth and even toned. She rarely needed makeup, and she surely didn't need mascara, she had thick stumpy lashes that looked like perfect little fans.

On the other hand, she had brown hair and not in a shade that was remarkable in her eyes either. She was going to put a rinse on it. She didn't like it. It was nowhere near as luxurious as Addi's.

Addi's hair was jet black, thick, long and looked like a lions mane when out. Whereas she had to use volumizing sprays and potions to have even half the body that Addi had. She resented her curls and would have gotten it processed a year ago except that her only time with a flat iron had her hair looking thin, long and lifeless more than she was comfortable with.

Addi was quite obviously the better looking of the two of them in her humble biased opinion. She made crossed eyes and pushed her tongue out at Addi. Then she felt like a cow for comparing herself to her cousin.

She slumped dramatically beside her.

"You are leaving because I am ugly aren't you?"

"Yes." Addi laughed. "I can't bear to see your ugly face anymore."

"And I have no boobs," Sky said despairingly.

Addi was in hysterics. "Yep. I am going to pursue an education away from here because you have no boobs."

"No Addi and no boyfriend." Sky groaned. "My life sucks."

"Your life is fine." Addi turned to Sky. "Stop feeling sorry for yourself. It's unattractive."

"I am unattractive," Sky muttered, "that's why I have nothing."

"You know very well that you are gorgeous." Addi shook her head in exasperation. "And you have your whole life ahead of you filled with glorious possibilities. I don't have a boyfriend and my life is quite fine."

"You don't have a boyfriend because you like Randy Vassell and nobody meets up to chocolate coated Randy." Sky stuck out her tongue at Addi. "You two were a thing in another time. Remember?"

"Shut up." Addi scowled. "I don't remember many details. I wrote stuff down but..."

"You wrote stuff down about you and Randy, but you didn't write about the fire or any significant financial details we should know!"

Addi nodded.

"I take it back," Sky said in exasperation. "You are not the mature one."

Addi inhaled, "I didn't think my memories of before were going to be relevant to us now. Everything changed for the family. You were the one with the financial details and all of that. There was no need for me to write down anything."

Sky grimaced. It was true. She had confidently assured Addi that she would take care of them financially with all of her information.

Look at her now. No book. No nothing.

"Randy doesn't talk to me anymore," Addi said defeat in her voice. "It is one of the reasons I am going too. He just stopped corresponding. He used to send me a card for my birthday. He doesn't anymore!"

"Because you told him to stop. There is just so much a guy can take. You pushed him away." Sky elbowed Addi. "Josh told me that he is working in Kingston as a junior accountant. Why don't you stay in Jamaica and go to a school in Kingston so that you can be near him? You guys could get it on again."

"Nope." Addi shook her head. "I am going to New York."

"Wrong, stupid answer." Sky got up. "I still think you are the worse yet."

Addi grinned. "I have a feeling by the end of the semester

when you find a boyfriend, and you get obsessed you'll be asking who is Addison again?"

"Not   likely,"   Sky   muttered.   "Not   at   all   likely."

Chapter Two

January 1996

"**H**eard they replaced old Dr. Mathers this year. There goes my easy A in International Marketing." Emma, her old roommate and now classmate said as she sat beside Sky. "The man was blind as a bat, and slightly senile. The university should be ashamed of themselves for letting him go, he was perfect!"

Sky laughed.

"So who is the new teacher?" Emma grunted as she slapped her knapsack on the desk. "I hope it's another senior citizen with sight problems."

"Don't know." Sky yawned and pulled her hoodie over her hair and crouched down further in her chair. "One Dr. Jefferson or something. Wake me up when he is done."

Emma chuckled. "Too much partying in the old year, huh?"

"No." Sky cracked one eye opened. "Well... a little. My

cousins came from New York, and I was very instrumental in planning my neighbor's wedding. The bride is a dressmaker, and we thought that we should do an elaborate dress. She looked gorgeous. It was fun."

"Good for you." Emma grimaced. "I flunked three courses last semester...have to take them over this year. My mother spent all Christmas talking about it. You would believe that I had murdered someone or something the way she kept carrying on."

"You were a little wild last year with the constant partying." Sky pointed out gently.

"I was not wild. I was a normal teenager with an unusual amount of freedom and like thinking friends." Emma huffed, "I don't know how you took ten courses."

"By not partying." Sky smirked, "and having zero social life. I want to get out of here. Not prolong the pain."

"You didn't fail any of the courses did you?" Emma asked hopefully.

"No." Sky shook her head, "A for every single one. Sorry to be so good at the school thing."

Emma snorted. "Yeah, you are forgiven. So where are you living this semester?"

"Off campus, in the town. My mother's relative has an apartment there. It's empty, so I got the go-ahead to live there and drive her car too."

"Cool." Emma widened her eyes. "Super cool. I wish I had a set up like that."

Sky nodded. "It's a nice place—two bedrooms. Each of them with their own bathroom. Bungalow style. Each apartment has a view of the pool at the back."

"That's totally wasted on you." Emma sighed, "I would have parties every weekend. Pool parties."

Sky shook her head. "No parties, unless the other residents

okay it. I am afraid it's not a place that's party friendly."

"That's totally your speed then." Emma straightened up when the classroom door opened and then widened her eyes in disappointment. "He's young and disabled!"

She spoke so loudly that the man who had wheeled himself into the classroom looked up to where they were sitting and nodded.

"Yes. I am disabled. Thank you for that observation Miss...?"

He was looking at her. Sky sat up straighter. "I er...It wasn't me."

"Okay, Miss It Wasn't Me."

The rest of the class chuckled.

He moved around to the desk putting a stack of books on it and then introduced himself. "My name is Travis Jefferson. I am sure I will get to know your names by the end of this semester."

Sky didn't dare make eye contact with him. She was feeling embarrassed. All through the first hour, she kept her head down.

Emma leaned in to whisper to her near the end of class. "This guy is fine. It's a pity he is in a wheelchair. How old do you think he is?"

"I don't know," Sky mumbled. "Stop talking."

Emma wasn't listening though. "Seriously Sky, he looks a little like an Indian Superman, don't you think? A dark honey Christopher Reeves with brown eyes. Look at the cowlick and the jawline. We have ourselves an undercover Superman."

"Shut up!" Sky growled a bit too loud.

Travis Jefferson looked up at them from his place in front of the class and then spun closer to the edge of the dais. "You have something to say to me, Miss It Wasn't Me?"

"No er..." Sky swallowed. He was pegging her for a troublemaker; Sky could see it in the narrowed gaze thrown at her.

She groaned inwardly. This was not going to be an A class for her. Superman hated her.

She vowed not to sit beside Emma for the rest of the semester. Maybe she would sit farther in the back.

****

Travis wheeled himself to his van, maneuvered himself on the ramp and secured his chair to the driver's side of the vehicle. He always felt a tinge of thankfulness when he thought about the freedom of driving a car for himself, living on his own and pursuing a career. A decade ago when he was bedridden, all of this was not an option.

A tap on his window had him winding it down and staring at the teacher outside. One year ago he would have eagerly wound down the window and smiled at her. Today he didn't; Amelia Perkins was on his list of persons to avoid.

"Hi Travis," she smiled at him. Her smile perfect. "We are having a get together at my place. It's a back to school kind of thing and a meet and greet for the new lecturers in our department. It's at eight. You remember where my place is don't you?"

"Yes," Travis nodded, "but I am afraid I can't make it. I have other plans."

"Are you in pain?" She asked concerned. Looking him over, pity in her eyes when she looked at his lifeless legs.

"No." Travis gritted his teeth. "Rich cripples can have plans too."

She gasped. "Travis, when are you going to allow me to forget that silly conversation from last year? I didn't mean it when I called you...a...cripple."

Travis grimaced. "I took no offense to that Amelia. It's the truth. What I took offense to was you inferring to your friend, Sandy, that I could be dateable because I am tied to the rich Jefferson's.

"You said, and I quote, 'Travis has two things going for him, the fact that he is good-looking at least from his waist up and his family's millions. Ooh, those millions, I would date a cripple to get close to those millions."

Amelia closed her eyes in mortification. "That wasn't a conversation I ever, ever wanted you to hear. We were just girls having fun saying stuff."

"I know." Travis nodded. "It's amazing the things you can hear when people don't know they are being listened to."

He wound up the window in her face and started the vehicle.

There was no denying it; he was still smarting from the overheard conversation. He backed out of the parking lot and wondered when he would stop feeling the twinge of hurt he felt when he heard Amelia discussing him with her friends so crassly.

To her, it had been last year, something to be dismissed. To him, it was just six weeks ago. And he was feeling particularly bad about the whole conversation because he had feelings for her.

He had been prepared to let her in, to trust her, to consider a relationship with her. That was a huge step for him. He hadn't had those thoughts about anyone for years.

He had thought that his heart had died with his legs. But it hadn't died; he had just chosen the wrong woman to consider offering it to.

He backed out of the parking lot and headed home to his apartment. He hadn't been lying to Amelia when he said that he had plans. It was his mother's birthday; he had to give her a call.

It was also his fifth year anniversary of being an independent adult. It had taken him years to convince his overprotective mother that he could live on his own.

Better than convincing his mother was convincing himself that he was worthy of the opportunity to be alive because he shouldn't be alive. It was his fault that he was in this wheelchair.

He often thought of his wheelchair as punishment for his sins. His prison.

All of the things that he had taken for granted before the wheelchair he was so appreciative for now.

He had not thought that his legs were a blessing until he lost the use of it. He missed some simple things, like running, or wriggling his toes in warm sand, or exercising and feeling his leg muscles burn.

Just feeling his legs would be good.

He turned the car into the apartment and greeted the security. Someone was parked in his parking place.

His space was right before his apartment. It was wider than usual so that he could maneuver his chair out of the van and straight to his door. He had chosen the corner apartment for that reason.

He didn't want to blow the horn; it was six in the evening. It would be inconsiderate to the other residents in the building.

But who would be so stupid as to park their car in the furthest spot from the rest of the parking spaces?

Who would be so utterly foolish that they would park in a space with an obvious disabled sign... he felt himself getting angry and then calmed down.

There were twelve apartments in the compound. Eleven of them were currently occupied. The apartment to the right of his was usually empty. For the five years, he had been living there he had met the owner once. A fast-talking lady named Corvette or was it, Yvette?

The door opened, and a girl stepped out in short shorts and a slouchy blue sweater.

He wound down the window. "Is this your car?"

She jumped and then turned to look at him like a deer caught in headlights.

"Yes," she nodded vigorously, "it is."

"Can you move it?" he asked impatiently. "It is in my parking space."

"Oh, sorry. I am so sorry, Sir!" she said a mortified tone to her voice, she moved closer to his side of the car and he saw that it was his student from today.

The pretty one, the loud one that he had called Miss It Wasn't Me. What was she doing here?

He hoped that she wasn't going to be living beside him. He didn't like having students in his space. They were usually noisy and untidy and didn't know how to respect boundaries.

And this one, he couldn't remember her name was obviously one of the popular outrageous ones. She had legs that went on for days, a smooth honey complexion and curly brown-red hair that she had styled in a casual topknot.

She probably would have a boyfriend coming over at various hours of the night and an assorted batch of girly friends crowding the swimming pool where he took his morning swim.

He watched as she backed out of his space and then he drove in. He waited for the ramp to be lowered and then he wheeled himself out and headed to his door.

She was parking in the proper designated area for her apartment. He waited for her to come out of the car.

Curiosity was getting the best of him. He had to find out

if she was going to be his neighbor. If she was, he had some ground rules to lay down. First one was not to park in his parking space.

She came out with a box in hand, slammed the car door and armed it.

"Sorry again Mr. er Dr, Jefferson. She wasn't making eye contact with him. She fiddled with the door and almost dropped her box.

He wheeled closer to her. "Let me help you with that." He indicated for the box, and she looked at him half scared.

"It's okay," he held out his hands. "I won't drop your box."

She reluctantly handed it to him and pushed the key into the door and opened it after two tries.

"So you'll be my neighbor?" He asked the obvious question. He had taken a look in the box. It was filled with cleaning supplies. She had probably just moved in.

"Yes," she said shyly. "My mom's cousin Yvette owns this place. She is gone to Italy for a while."

"I see." Travis nodded. "What's your name again? I had four new classes today. Quite a few names to remember and since you are going to be my neighbor I can't keep calling you, Miss It Wasn't Me."

"My name is Skyler Porter," She said smiling at him. "I really didn't mean to..."

"That's okay Miss Porter. Apology accepted. I hope I won't have any problems with you being my close neighbor. I hate loud noise and parties. The walls are not as thick as I would like."

"Oh no, I don't do parties," Sky said hurriedly, "I study a lot. I don't have a social life."

"We'll see." Travis handed her the box and wheeled himself to his door. "Have a good evening Miss Porter."

"You too, Dr. Jefferson," She said quickly. He heard when

she closed the door. He suppressed a laugh—she only studied and didn't have a social life. Yeah right.

Chapter Three

Sky spent most of the first week back at school flitting from class to class without a breather. In the nights she cleaned the apartment room by room. Yvette had not had anyone clean it for what seemed like years. The furniture had layers of dust, the bedding and sheets were musty and the refrigerator, though it looked new was not working.

She had three different repairmen coming by to look at it. The last one, a cocky, self-assured guy named Brian, who looked a lot like the boxer Mike Tyson, announced to her that it was an easy fix.

He flirted with her mercilessly and obscenely smacked his lips when he spoke to her. Thankfully, he solved the mystery of the refrigerators malady. Though she nodded while he elaborated on the mysterious problem, she had no clue what he was talking about.

All she could think was, *why on earth didn't he hurry and leave?*

She let him out of her place close to midnight on Friday night, after he tinkered with the back of the fridge and got it working again.

She was very grateful to him for the fix, and even more grateful when she heard what he was charging. She paid him quickly, all the while thinking of all the things that she was deprived of because she did not have a fridge for a week.

She could cook and have leftovers and drink cool water, and she could have her chocolate bars rock hard instead of room temperature.

"Say, want us to do something tonight?" Brian intruded on her thoughts.

He was standing too close when she let him out of the apartment. Sky hadn't even realized it at the time. The guy had no concept of personal space.

His casual invitation to go out with him was not welcomed. What on earth made him think that she would be willing to go anywhere with him?

"No, I am good," she said briskly.

Brian scowled. "What's wrong with you? You don't like blue collar workers?"

"I just don't want to go out with you." Sky scowled back at him. "I had a stressful week at school. All I want to do now is go inside, put my chocolate bar in the fridge and wait for it to harden and then eat it...slowly."

Brian laughed. "I like you."

Sky rolled her eyes. This guy was not going to take any rejection of him seriously.

"I would probably like you if you weren't coming on so strongly."

"It's my thing, you know." Brian winked. "I see a pretty girl like you I just have to get a word in, make myself memorable."

Sky considered rolling her eyes and then decided not to. Brian looked as if he had a chip on his shoulder a mile wide and he looked as if rejecting him with a no would not cut it.

Sky sighed. "I have a boyfriend, Brian. I can't go out with you."

"Who?" Brian asked crossing his arms over his chest and showing off his bulging biceps.

Sky considered going inside and slamming the door in his face, but she had a funny feeling that this level of persistence would not be solved with a simple slam of the door. She imagined he would keep coming back and hounding her to go out with him.

"Why do you want to know who?" Sky asked frowning. "How is that any of your business?"

"Because women lie," Brian said smugly, "and if you really don't have a guy, you are fair game. I like you. I am going to pursue you, wear you down. You'll see what a great guy I am when I am done."

Sky shuddered, and it wasn't from the chilly January night. It was the thought of Brian hounding her, maybe for the next year and a half that she would be living in Mount Faith. She wracked her brain for a name. She didn't have any single guy friends.

"I don't think I should tell you," she tried hedging, "he's ah..."

"Married?" Brian asked raising an eyebrow.

"No." Sky frowned, "he's ah..."

"Invisible?" Brian was enjoying watching her squirm.

Sky looked out at the parking lot in front of the house in defeat and then she spotted Travis Jefferson's van.

Emma had been going on and on about him all week. She had even found a ridiculous article about people in wheelchairs and sex. *"If you live beside him, Sky, you must find out if he's all there, down there. I wouldn't mind dating him. I don't care if he's in a wheelchair."*

Sky looked at Brian and smirked. "I'd prefer not to say his name because he is a lecturer at my school."

"Oh." Brian nodded and then laughed, "nice try."

"I am serious." Sky hissed, "he lives next door, and he wouldn't like me talking to you so long out here. Now go, before he sees you."

Brian chuckled. "Likely story."

Sky inhaled. "Goodnight Brian. Thank you for fixing my fridge." She was about to close the door when Brian put his foot on the threshold.

"Not so fast. I was thinking we could go out tomorrow. Spend the day together. You know. Get to know each other better."

"No!" Sky said firmly, "leave me alone. Now!"

"Or else what?" Brian sneered, "Your boyfriend from next door will come to your rescue?"

Sky felt real fear at the look of determination in Brian's eyes. He was acting way past creepy.

She almost slumped on the wall in relief when she heard the door from next door open. And then she heard Travis Jefferson's voice.

"Sky, is everything all right?"

He had never called her Sky before, always Miss Porter.

"No," she almost pushed Brian out of the way and stood in the corridor,

He was dressed all in black his hair was ruffled more than usual. He looked at Brian with a frown. "What are you doing here?"

"Nothing," Brian straightened up guiltily, "I... er... thought that Sky was... er... single. I had no idea she was telling the truth. Listen, man; I don't trample on other men's territory.

I am a lover, not a fighter. This is just a misunderstanding. Goodnight."

He walked stiffly to his car and then drove out.

Sky slumped on the wall and sighed. "Such a pity he is borderline dangerous. I think he is a good electrician. He's the only one who knew how to fix my fridge. Thank you, Dr. Jefferson."

Travis nodded. "No problem. That's what boyfriends are for, and he is dangerous not just borderline."

"You heard the conversation?" Sky groaned, "I am so sorry. I couldn't think of anyone to use as my imaginary boyfriend. I saw your van and..."

"No worries." Travis wheeled back to his apartment. "Goodnight Miss Porter."

They were back to her being Miss Porter.

"Goodnight Dr. Jefferson." She straightened up from the wall.

****

For a full month, Sky watched as he swam in the mornings. She watched as he pulled himself out of the water and into his special chair. She was fascinated with him. She had turned into a low-key stalker.

She could probably memorize his schedule by now. He swam every morning at six without fail. Her back patio gave a clear view of the pool.

She could time the squeak of his wheelchair as it progressed along the pool lounge area. There was a special place at the end of the pool where he stopped and lowered himself from his chair and into the water.

The first morning she saw him entering the pool she got anxious like a mother hen, waiting to see if he could manage all by himself. She didn't have long to wait. He was an expert at it. She felt ridiculous after that.

When had she gotten so invested in him?

The following morning she observed a couple of details as she watched him. His chair was different from the one he rode to class. He wore black swimming trunks, his legs were skinnier than his upper body, but his upper body was rippling with muscles.

When he hauled himself from the water with the help of the rails, he always gave a glance at her section of the apartment like he knew she was watching.

She dismissed that idea after the first week. He didn't know she was watching. He didn't have the same kind of madness that was infecting her.

He had breakfast at seven thirty. She heard him in the kitchen banging around. He liked to listen to the BBC World News for half an hour and then he played music. He liked stuff like Enya, Sail Away and Sail On by the Commodores. He played it constantly.

She could hear it, especially when he opened his patio doors. She concluded that he had a thing for sailing.

He left for school at nine, most days, except for Wednesdays.

She watched him at school. She couldn't believe that she had not seen him before her class with him. He was truly a lovely looking man.

And she was reminded of that every class because she had not quite managed to shake Emma who seemed to be as obsessed as she was becoming about him.

Wherever she sat, Emma was there with little tidbits of information.

"I found out his age!" Emma announced in mid-January. "He is thirty-one."

A week later she announced, "I know how and why he met

in the accident that crippled him," Emma had told her almost panting with glee at the announcement. "I have all the scoop on him. All the scoop!"

Sky had pretended that she didn't want to hear, but she had found herself traipsing behind Emma as she headed to the cafeteria like an obedient puppet and playing as if she was nonchalant while Emma scarfed down her burger and fries and told her some silly story about a party that had gone wrong.

"About Dr. Jefferson?" Sky snapped in the middle of Emma's telling. "I have to go to another class."

"Dr. Jefferson." Emma looked at her smugly. "You came here for Dr. Jefferson, didn't you? Not to have lunch with me."

Sky would have gotten up then and stormed off, but her curiosity was heightened. She had wondered more than once how he got injured, so she swallowed the retort at the tip of her tongue and glared at Emma.

"Yes, I want to hear about Dr. Jefferson." She didn't know if her voice could be any more longsuffering.

Emma cackled. "Good girl. It is time you admit that you think he is the finest lecturer here, wheelchair or not."

"I admit it," Sky growled.

"Now before I give you any details, you have to promise me something."

"What?" Sky looked at Emma, her eyes narrowed.

"Please, please, please let me come over to your place for the weekend. My current roommate is driving me nuts. She talks too much, she has boyfriend issues, and she is constantly hogging the phone. I just want a break. Besides, I can get to see gorgeous Dr. J. all weekend. What does he do on the weekend?"

Sky gritted her teeth. "No."

"Yes." Emma grinned. "Because I am not telling you what I know until you help me."

"Okay." Sky closed her eyes and then opened them. She was going to regret having Emma over for the weekend. All the reasons why she had a problem with her roommate were identical to problems she had had with her. "Okay."

"Well," Emma said moving into storytelling mode, her eyes lit with glee. "I called a friend of mine in Kingston who knows everything about everyone, and I was telling her that I had a crush on my teacher, Dr. Jefferson. And girl, let me tell you, I have enough information to fill a magazine."

"Really?" Sky asked skeptically.

"Don't interrupt." Emma grinned. "You'll love this. So, hear this, Travis Jefferson is rich. I mean rich, like crazy rich. His father is Miguel Jefferson of the pharmaceutical Jefferson's. The guy has a Caribbean empire. Anyway, Travis is his prized only son. He has like two or three older sisters or something.

"Anyway, Travis was reportedly wild. You know the kind of wild I am talking about—lots of girls, drinking and all of that jazz. He was on his father yacht one day, a couple of years ago, and some friends of his challenged him to a water ski race. Rumor has it that Travis was drunk; the guy who challenged him was drunk too, and they had some love rival or something.

"They raced then collided. Rumor has it that the collision was not an accident, that somebody tampered with the jet skis. Anywho, Travis was crippled, and his frenemy and love rival damaged his brain. That is why Dr. J Hotty is in a wheelchair."

"Oh," Sky nodded, "thanks for telling me."

"There's more," Emma said rubbing her hands together, "a juicy bit more."

"What?" Sky was so interested she was leaning toward Emma like a dutiful puppy waiting for the next morsel.

"He and a professor here had a thing last year, and they broke up."

"Which professor?" Sky asked feeling odd. Why hadn't she thought of him having relationships?

"The economics lady, the one who looks a little like Malinda Williams in that movie, A Thin Line Between Love and Hate. And she dresses like a runway model. Always matching."

"Miss Perkins," Sky whispered. "And I haven't seen the movie yet. It's not out in local theatres yet. How did you even watch it?"

"Doesn't matter," Emma said smugly. "What is important here is that Dr. Jefferson is functional. Miss Perkins looks like the type that would care about that."

"You are something else." Sky got up.

"See you this weekend." Emma winked at her. "I am taking my bathing suits."

Chapter Four

"**T**his one or this one?" Emma came to her room door and held up two bathing suits. "I am going to meet Dr. Hotty at the poolside."

Sky peered over the sheet at Emma and groaned. "Go away."

"You know you want to join us." Emma chuckled. "Yesterday you watched him like you were starving. I saw it, don't deny it. I can't understand why you are so shy."

Sky covered her head with the blankets and listened as Emma walked away. She heard the door to the patio open and Emma's flirty laugh as she approached the pool.

She had arrived for her weekend stay from Friday. And had spent all the weekend trying to chat up Travis at the pool. When she wasn't trying to get Travis' attention, she was eating all her groceries for the week.

Sky inhaled ruggedly. That's what she got for being curious about Travis Jefferson. Emma would thankfully be gone in six hours. She had a group meeting for a project. Then Sky would have the apartment to herself. She was never going to bargain for information again. She closed her eyes trying to shut out Emma's laugh as she recounted some story or the other to Travis.

He never laughed back, and the conversation seemed one-sided. Good. Sky thought jealously. She wished she was as bold as Emma, but she was not. She would never be. She was cured of all girlish nonsense like crushes.

Her last crush, Rusty, had been a disaster.

Not only had he been her mother's secret lover but things could have ended up much worse if her cousin had not changed events. She could have given up her virginity to Rusty. The very thought was horrifying.

Rusty was the man who would have killed her father had Addi not intervened.

Worse than that, she had spent her future obsessed with him. What could be more dismal and psychologically screwed up than obsessing over the guy who killed your father?

She hadn't said this to anybody, but she was concerned that she couldn't trust herself to make good decisions. Since she heard about the decisions that she had made in another time, she was teetering on the edge of clinical self-doubt. So this fascination with her neighbor, her current lecturer was probably another bad idea.

But when she closed her eyes his face came up in her mind's eye. She was tormented about him. It was like madness. She wasn't sure that this was on the scale like a crush she briefly had for Rusty.

She got up and held her head in her hands. She assessed herself honestly. What was it that she found so fascinating about Travis Jefferson?

He was handsome, yes. A fairly good lecturer, yes. He was

strict with assignment dates, and he had a sadistic streak where he gave them surprise exams. There was something about him that she found attractive. She didn't know what it was and it was driving her nuts.

Maybe it was just regular teenage hormones chipping in after a long four-year break. Her nineteenth birthday had come and gone at the end of January, and she had escaped the usual pitfalls of attraction to another person.

And what a person she had chosen to be fixated on. A man that was unavailable. A man that was older than her by quite a bit, not that it was majorly significant but still... And she couldn't forget that he was physically disabled. She had never taken much notice of people in wheelchairs before Travis Jefferson.

This, whatever it was, would pass.

It had to.

She turned on her radio and headed for the bathroom. She needed to wash her thoughts away, sing at the top of her voice, start the day fresh. She usually felt energized after doing that.

Sunday morning oldies belted from her radio. She sang aloud to The Supremes, Baby Love, and then You Can't Hurry Love.

She exited the shower and wiped the steam from the glass and picked up her brush pretending to be Diana Ross. *You can't hurry love oh you just have to wait...*

A little mad streak had her dancing along and pretending she was eight again and entertaining the family with Addi as her faithful sidekick.

She finished with her antics when the song ended. She dried off and headed for the closet, which still housed some of Yvette's clothes. Clothes, which Yvette had casually, said Sky should wear or give away.

She had turned Sundays into Yvette's Clothes Day. Some of the outfits were very nice, others were weird, like the black jumper suit that was littered with pointy sequins that was dangerous to handle much less wear. Where had Yvette worn it?

Sky took out a simple soft gray cashmere dress, which hugged her body in the right places and made her look like she had curves. It had long bell sleeves and stopped at her knees. This would be today's dress, though it was nice enough to wear to school.

She let her hair down and put some moisturizer on it, hoping that it wouldn't dry out and become frizzy. Her hair hung down her back in little red-brown curly tendrils. Her real hair color was growing back from the roots with a vengeance and snaring at her attempts to hide it.

She gave her hair a little flash and headed to the living room.

Emma came racing in, her eyes dancing in excitement. "He invited us to breakfast!"

Emma squealed. "I don't know why, but he said you should come along. I tried to tell him that you were sleeping, but unfortunately, you were singing so loud that the whole Malvern could hear you. Why were you singing at the top of your voice like that?"

"Breakfast?" Sky was on her way to the settee.

She froze. "In his apartment?"

"Yes." Emma ran to the guest room, "I am going to dress to the nines!"

Sky sat down abruptly. Breakfast? She was finally going to see inside his apartment and eating with him. What kind of stranglehold did Emma have on Travis Jefferson that she could wring this kind of invitation from him?

****

Travis closed his eyes in exhaustion when he entered his apartment after his swim. He had never had such a stressful morning in all of his thirty-one years. Fending off a chattering, perplexing teenaged female had all but wrung him out. The chattering he could handle, but when Emma had walked into his apartment, apparently looked into his fridge and then declared that she would come over and fix him breakfast.

That had been too much.

He had considered yelling for security or squeezing the panic button that was on his chair.

Thankfully, he had come to his senses before overreacting. He had managed to see the light side to Emma's behavior. She wasn't sinister in any way. She probably weighed a little over a hundred pounds. Coupled with her overly bright smile, she looked like a pixie.

She wouldn't do him any bodily harm; she just had no concept of boundaries. She barreled in where others were afraid to go.

He didn't want the security thinking he was a wuss that couldn't handle a girl with a crush.

The other option was to tell her firmly to leave him alone, but that had not worked yesterday. She had gone blessedly silent and then started talking again.

So instead of vinegar, he was trying honey. He had invited her to breakfast, told her he liked to prepare it himself and asked her to bring Sky with her. Sky was supposed to act as a buffer. In the six weeks that Sky was his neighbor, he had not had any occasion to complain about her.

She was silent as a mouse except when she sang in the shower. She had a pretty nice voice he couldn't complain about her singing.

Except for that encounter with the persistent electrician, a couple of weeks ago, he hardly saw her outside of class.

Last week was the first time he had seen her on campus. She was sitting in the Greens on a picnic blanket talking animatedly to a mixed group of people. There were more guys in the group than girls. He hadn't missed the look that the guy to her right was giving her. He had been staring at her with adoration. Sky seemed to have that effect on men.

He had stopped and watched her for a while. If he were to be honest, he was curious about her. He had greatly misjudged her based on her looks. He had instantly summed her up as a party girl who probably had more than one boyfriend.

Sky had debunked his theories—he had given his class two exams so far, and she had completed them with grades in the nineties, and she had no visitors, male or female.

Emma had just chirpily told him that Sky was dating her books and that she had more than the usual course load this semester.

He hated when people judged him based on the fact that he was in a wheelchair and yet he had had no problems summing up Sky after an initial meeting. He was remorseful about that. One thing was for sure, he was quite happy she was his neighbor and not Emma Brown.

He wheeled himself into the shower and turned it on warm.

His whole apartment was refitted for his needs; he had bought the place and extensively remodeled it. Counters were to his height; the shower was retrofitted to accommodate a wheelchair. His whole life was on a different level literally.

What would take him ten minutes before, when he was on his feet, like taking a bath and getting dressed, now took him at least thirty minutes.

He showered quickly and pulled on a pair of specially designed jeans and then his grey sweater. It had been the usually cool morning. By the time he had brushed his hair and teeth and wheeled into the kitchen, it was eight o'clock.

He wasn't terribly pleased to hear Emma knocking on his patio door shortly after he had decided that cereal, toast, eggs and orange juice was all he was willing to exert himself over this morning.

His helper cooked him good wholesome dinners in the week, on the weekends he didn't pretend that he was a chef. Takeout from a lovely mom and pop restaurant around the corner usually sufficed and barring that he went light with his selections.

He reluctantly wheeled to the door and opened it, letting in an overeager Emma who was dressed as if she was going to a party. She was in a short pink dress and sky-high heels with a face full of heavy makeup.

He suppressed a groan. What he should have done after the swim was, come inside and lock the door and not answer the knock when he saw that it was Emma. He changed his mind almost instantly as Sky appeared behind her.

"Good morning, Dr. Jefferson." She held up a bottle of juice, the same type he was about to remove from his fridge. "I brought juice to contribute to... er... this invite."

"Good morning, Sky," he smiled at her taking in her simple dress her make-up free face that was beaming with health and her flip-flops. She was a breath of fresh air compared to Emma.

"So TJ what are you fixing?" Emma had gone straight to the kitchen, flitting about as if she owned it.

He looked at Sky. "Don't tell me she is going to be living next door?"

Sky shook her head. "Five hours till leaving time."

"And no more weekends, please," Travis whispered. "Or I'll have to call security or take out a restraining order."

Sky laughed.

"What are you two whispering about?" Emma came around her high heels clicking on the floor.

Travis wheeled toward Emma and scowled. "I know you are hard of hearing, but if you call me TJ ever again, you will pay."

Emma recoiled. He could see that she was finally taking him seriously. But then he felt really bad for saying it, but he didn't dare take it back.

She withdrew like a puppy that had been freshly kicked, and he had to admit he felt a sense of relief at that.

****

Emma's withdrawal did not last long. She started calling him Dr. Jefferson again, and she dominated the breakfast conversation.

He served breakfast at the nook, which was closest to where he prepared the food. That had taken record time. He was incentivized to get Emma out of his apartment.

And now he knew much more about her than he wanted. He knew her favorite color, the name of her favorite childhood dog, and her family's little foibles. He concluded before he got the telephone call that would put breakfast to an end that Emma was a spoiled young woman.

Sky's only contribution to the running dialogue was a yes here or there when Emma stopped to catch her breath.

He found himself wishing that Sky was the talkative one, that she was the one who had a crush on him and couldn't wait to have breakfast in his place. He wondered what her story was.

He guessed that his behavior mirrored Sky's until two curious things happened. His phone rang, and he held up his hand to stem Emma's one-man conversation.

Sky looked at his hands and gasped.

He had no idea what that overreaction was about. Emma stopped talking long enough for him to point to the living room.

"My phone is ringing," he said wheeling away to the shrieking phone.

It was Amelia. He had never thought of Amelia in terms of being a savior. She was the woman who had unwittingly stirred his romantic hopes for a while, but now he had never been so grateful to hear her voice.

"Hi," her tone was bashful. He had never heard Amelia do bashful before.

"Hello Amelia," He replied evenly. Normally he would scowl, but today he was going to use her call as an excuse to get Emma away from his place. Later when she was gone, he would query about that gasp from Sky.

"I was just calling to er...ask if you wanted to come over for dinner or maybe I could bring dinner to your place."

Amelia was looking for absolvement, and he had pouted long enough. What she had said was not as devastating as he had thought it had been just a few months ago. So what if she had said, that she would date a cripple to get close to his family's money.

People said things. Besides, he had no desire to pursue a relationship with Amelia anymore. Somehow it had gone. He had lost that loving feeling.

"Travis, are you there?"

"Yes um, yes. Fine. I'll come over," He said huskily then cleared his throat. "What time?"

"Is two too early?"

"Not at all." He hung up the phone and turned to see Sky and Emma watching him.

"Sorry ladies," he said. "I have to be somewhere. I will see you in class tomorrow."

Sky jumped up quickly and was already heading to the door before he could give any more hints. Emma took a longer time to get up. She looked woebegone.

"I er, well Dr. Jefferson, thank you for breakfast."

"You are welcome." Travis nodded. "Don't forget the test tomorrow. It will be challenging."

He delivered the last salvo hoping that Emma would keep her distance in their future classes.

She nodded and left.

He inhaled deeply and made sure that he pulled back the back patio blinds. He was taking no chances with Emma around.

Chapter Five

"**I** didn't know Dr. Hotty and Amelia Perkins were still together," Emma mourned. "Do you think that is why he was giving me the cold shoulder? I feel like such a fool."

Sky was sprawled out on the sofa her head in a business textbook. She hadn't heard a word Emma had said for the past hour. She was biding her time until Emma left. As soon as she closed the door; she was going to call Addi.

When Travis held up his hands today, she saw that he had just two lines in the hand he held up. That was the mark of a resetter. Wasn't that the same marking that Addi had in her palms before she traveled back to 1992?

"Are you even listening to me?" Emma sat across from Sky and pouted.

Sky looked up at her and shook her head. "To be honest, I tuned you out a long time ago. Just let the whole thing with Travis Jefferson go. He is not the type to give you a good grade because you flirted with him."

"Do you think that is why I spent all weekend trying to get to know him?" Emma pouted.

"Isn't it?" Sky raised an eyebrow.

"No!" Emma gasped. "I really, really like him. Well, maybe I thought that if we had a thing I could get a better grade, but that was a while ago. The truth is, I have never been with a guy in a wheelchair. I was curious about that."

"Ah," Sky nodded, "I see. You are a creature of impulse and adventure."

"Yes." Emma beamed. "I like how you put it—impulse and adventure. Sounds good. That's what I am."

Sky shook her head. "You know, you can't go through university like this? At some point, you are going to have to focus and get serious. You will eventually have to put some of your efforts into actual work, or else you'll be up here forever repeating courses, and as one group of your friends come and go, you'll be stuck. You'll probably graduate when you are thirty!"

Emma snorted and then got up. "Well thanks for the pop psychology, Missy. In my opinion, you are the one that needs to lighten up. You only live once. There is a place for a social life at school."

"I agree," Sky said, "but in moderation and not at the expense of your schoolwork. Education is an expensive investment, and it's foolhardy trying to cut corners by flirting with your lecturers or trying to exploit their vulnerabilities. You thought that he was fair game because he was in a wheelchair."

"You know what, I am leaving. There is no use hanging around here with you, Miss Doom and Gloom. I am going to hang with Sher and the others." Emma flounced to the guest room.

"By the way, you suck at the flirting thing. You are more

annoying than alluring." Sky said to her retreating back.

Emma looked back at her balefully. "Not true, you are just jealous of me and my ease with people and the fact that I have a gazillion friends and I go to the best parties."

Sky widened her eyes and then laughed.

"Laugh all you want," Emma said, "but the whole point of university is having social contacts. It means I can get a job that much easier than you Miss Perfect GPA. Maybe one day I'll even be your boss because I know the right people."

Sky nodded. "I see. If you are going to be my boss, I might as well be nice to you from now. Want me to drop you back at school?"

"Sure," Emma said still sounding a little put off by Sky.

****

After dropping Emma at the dormitory, Sky thought about what she said earlier. She had to work on her social life. She had left high school a year earlier than most of her friends and had started at Mount Faith friendless. Most of the people she associated with, were mature people, serious about their school work. And they were competitive. If you wanted to keep just ahead of them, you had to put in the extra reading.

She wasn't going to feel sorry for the fact that she wasn't repeating classes and went to the best parties.

She was on track to graduate in '97. That's how she wanted it. She didn't need friends. She had Addi.

Her cousin would have to suffice. She pulled into her parking space beside Travis' van. He hadn't left for his date yet.

She ignored the pang of jealousy that she felt when she thought about it and headed for the door.

Travis' door opened at the same time she pushed her key

into her door's lock.

She heard the whirring of the wheelchair as he entered the corridor. She looked over at him to say hello, and he looked around her cautiously.

"Is she gone?"

"Yes." Sky nodded. "Just dropped her by her dorm. Sorry about her this weekend. She really is harmless."

Travis exhaled. "I can't understand how you two are friends."

Sky swallowed. "It's complicated. We were roommates last semester. She said she had some information that I wanted to hear. Staying over for the weekend was the exchange."

"Information?" Travis raised an eyebrow. They were thick and level and neat. Sky found herself wondering idly how his grew so neatly when she had to shape up hers every two weeks.

"You have time for a visit?" Travis indicated his door.

Sky nodded jerkily. "Yes."

"You sure I am not taking you from your studies. I am giving you a test tomorrow."

"Very sure." Sky grinned. "Your course is easy."

Travis grinned. "Well, come over then."

Sky followed him and then closed the door behind them. The apartment had the same layout as hers—Open plan living room, leading to the patio. If his blinds weren't drawn, you could see the pool.

The kitchen was at the side with a nook area. As she had noticed earlier though, everything was at a lower level to accommodate him.

"Have a seat." Travis indicated to one of his plush burgundy sofas.

Sky sat down. As she had noticed earlier, the color scheme was burgundy and cream. He had loads of plants. When she was there earlier she had thought that they looked unreal but now she looked closer; the one on the center table was very much real. It had red and pink flowers.

"That's a kalanchoe, Travis said pointing to it. "And that one too."

He pointed to a large vase at the patio door that had thick white flowers spilling over the top.

"They are gorgeous," Sky said. "When I came in earlier with Emma I thought that they were unreal especially your peace lilies. The leaves are so shiny."

Travis smiled. "Are you a plant lover too?"

"Well, yes. I like looking at other people's plants, and I do love to go to flower shows."

Travis nodded. "I do too. When I was younger, maybe twelve or so, I would take numerous photos of flowers. He moved over to the bookshelf and pulled out an album. Those were my hobbies—flowers and photography."

Sky took the album from him and skipped through. It seemed like each plant was better than the next. She was in the middle of the album when she felt his eyes on her. She looked up and smiled.

"What is it?"

"Earlier you gasped while Emma was talking. What was that about?"

Sky closed the album slowly an cleared her throat. "I just saw your palms, that's all."

"What about them?" Travis held them up and looked at it and then he turned it over so that Sky could see it.

Both of them had just two distinct lines, like a perfect 't'. One straight line from his index finger almost to his wrist and the other traveled across it to both ends of his palms.

No other lines criss-crossed these lines. Even his fingers were free of lines. It was fascinating to see.

Addi had told her that she was the one who spotted her palms in the previous timeline. She didn't know how she had managed to keep that a secret because this looked amazing.

Sky held up her hands because Travis was looking at her quizzically. "My hands have more lines than yours. Most people's hands have more lines."

Travis chuckled. "So you read tea leaves and think there are special powers in crystals too?"

"No." Sky shook her head. "Not at all. I just...Nothing."

Travis was watching her suspiciously. "You sure it's nothing?

"Sure." Sky nodded and then changed her mind about telling him.

What would it hurt if he knew? "I just heard that people with a 't' in their hands like yours can time travel."

Travis chuckled. "Okay."

"To the past only but they have to be connected with a pathway."

"A pathway." Travis nodded, "which would be..."

"A rock of some sort." Sky subsided in the chair. "I can see the incredulity in your eyes."

Travis nodded. "I never pegged you for a science fiction fan. I would think more romance and drama."

Sky grimaced. "Well, this is not fiction, but you are right. I am more of a romance and drama kind of girl. I love historical stuff though."

Travis moved toward his bookcase. "Well, behold, my paperback collection."

Sky jumped up and walked toward his bookshelf. Half of the large bookcase had historical romance paperback books."

"You have quite the library!" She looked up at him. "If I lived with you I wouldn't get anything done."

Travis' eyes darkened momentarily as if he were

contemplating it and then he smiled. "You can borrow one book at a time if you feel like it."

"Yes, thanks." Sky nodded. And then she moved away and back to the settee. "Since you love to read I have a set of diaries to lend you. Well, my cousin had them. I am going to have to call her and find out if she left them at home. She is in New York at the moment."

"Where is home?" Travis asked.

"I live in Mandeville, an hour from here."

"And your parents?"

"Divorced. My dad remarried our next door neighbor, and they have a son," Sky said contemplatively. "I guess I have no home."

"Why'd you say that?"

"I mean, I have a house where I go to for midterm or summer holidays, but a home implies warmth, family togetherness." Sky sighed. "When I go home I stay at my parent's old house. When I get lonely, I go to my uncle and aunt's, but they are hardly home. They spend a good chunk of their time in America. It is what it is."

Travis smiled. "I understand. My siblings from my father's first marriage would say the same thing when they came over to our house. My mother was a particularly nice stepmother by the way."

"Oh," Sky gasped, "I didn't know this about you!"

"What do you know about me?" Travis queried with a chuckle. "Who's your source?"

Sky hung her head in embarrassment. "Well, I...Emma. That is why I allowed her to spend the weekend, in exchange for information on you."

Travis laughed. "Now this puts me at an unfair disadvantage Skyler. I know nothing about you, and I have no idea what Emma told you."

"Well, it wasn't anything much." Sky felt uncomfortable. She avoided looking at him. "I was curious that's all."

"Because I am your neighbor and I lecture you currently," Travis nodded. "I get it."

"Yes!" Sky quickly hopped onto his excuse. Of course, she wouldn't admit that there was more—that she was attracted to him.

"Tell you what," Travis wheeled closer to her and held out her hand. "We agree to become friends…satisfy our curiosity about each other, be neighborly. No more agreements with Emma. Deal?"

"Yes, deal." Sky looked at his palms before she held out her hands and they touched. She looked up at him and then smiled.

He was an honest to goodness resetter, and he didn't even know it.

****

Sky called Addi as soon as she stepped into her apartment. She waited impatiently while the phone rang. Where could Addi be on a Sunday at one? She looked at the clock impatiently.

She hung up the phone and tried again. She had a limited amount of phone credit on her WorldTalk card. Addi had better answer this time.

"Hello," Addi answered groggily.

"My neighbor has a 't' in his palms!" Sky said excitedly. She didn't bother with hello. "A 't' Addi, no other lines, just a 't'. Isn't that a time travel thing?"

"Yes," Addi said sounding brighter. "You are sure it was a 't'?"

"Yes. Yes and yes!" Sky sank down on the settee, feeling

like she had discovered a new world. "He is also my teacher. I can't believe that I met a resetter in person. I mean, before they reset anything. I mean, apart from you obviously."

"That's great!" Addi enthused. "I wish I could meet him too. Is he planning to travel back?"

"No," Sky grunted. "I told him and he laughed at me… probably thinks I am touched in the head."

"If he goes back tell him to write stuff down. I wish I wrote stuff down when I just got back. You begin to lose the memories pretty quickly."

"I don't think he is going to go back. I mentioned time travel and pathways he thought it was fictional. I was thinking, did you leave Monica's grandmother's books at home?"

Addi paused. "Yes, I did. In my room. I meant to carry them, but I didn't get the chance. Too many things to take back with me whenever I visit home."

"Good," Sky said brightly. "I'll just go home for them one weekend and give them to him to read. Maybe he'll find it interesting."

"I hope so." Addi yawned. "But then again, I don't know, telling him about this could be more trouble than it is worth. What kind of person is he?"

"He is fine." Sky cleared her throat. "Like really fine. You only see his type of fine, rarely."

Addi laughed. "You like him!"

"Yes," Sky muttered, "but he is my lecturer."

"Older guy!" Addi chuckled. "You have a type."

"Don't remind me about my one, and I have to stress *one* crush before this." Sky sighed. "Travis Jefferson is not in any category of men I have been exposed to before. For one he is so mature and knowledgeable."

Addi laughed. "He is your teacher, duh. I would fret if he were immature and stupid."

Sky ignored her. "Two, he is in a wheelchair. I don't know anything about people in wheelchairs, except what crazy Emma has been feeding me about them."

"He is in a wheelchair?" Addi gasped. "Is he in a wheelchair because of a genetic condition?"

"No," Sky said massaging her temples, "What does that have to do with anything."

"Maybe he would like the chance to reset the event that crippled him in the first place. That would be nice."

"Splendid idea except he does not believe in this kind of thing, remember?"

"Josh didn't either," Addi reminded her, "and he came around, not to mention the fact that you took some convincing too. It takes time to make people come around."

"Yeah, I guess," Sky muttered. "Talk to you soon. I have to study for a test tomorrow."

"Okay." Addi yawned again. "Me too."

Chapter Six

Travis drove to Amelia's place wishing that he had never agreed to have dinner with her. He was quite pleased to see on arriving at the sprawling ranch-style house that there were several cars parked in the driveway. He had assumed that dinner would have been a private affair.

He parked closest to the door, maneuvered himself along the walkway, and headed to the front door. Amelia's mother answered the door and greeted him with a fake exuberance that he always found grating. She spoke to him as if he was hard of hearing instead of crippled.

"Oh how delightful, it's Travis!" She opened the door wider for him to wheel through. Amelia was from a large family— five brothers and two sisters. Two of the five brothers were pharmacists. He hoped they weren't the ones there.

They were, understandably, quite fascinated with his father's Pharmaceutical Company and asked him a million and one questions he was ill-equipped to answer.

The chief interrogator, Ancel, was the first one he saw when he entered the house. He almost groaned audibly. And then he saw Kenton, the journalist, and he did groan.

Amelia laughed and came over to him. She was dressed in a white pantsuit and looked quite attractive. Her arms were toned. Her pixie cut enhanced her bone structure, and as usual, she had that perfect smile.

"I am so sorry about this. I wanted this to be a brunch with just the two of us." She stooped so that they were almost eye-to-eye. "But my mother thought that this was the perfect moment to have an impromptu family get together. I will ask Kenton not to hound you for a story."

"Thank you." Travis dredged up a smile from somewhere.

He knew Kenton would be on his case. After all, tomorrow was the anniversary of his monumental mistake. The day when he had made the news and not in a positive way. Any journalist worth his salt would be delighted to have him as a dinner guest, to rehash his past, to compare his current situation with how he used to be, to hold him up as some sort of reformed playboy who had gotten his just desserts.

Everybody liked a redemption story and a cautionary tale.

Most people would like to hear that the rich kid with the world at his feet that had taken advantage of every vice known to man was now humbled in a wheelchair, teaching college kids and living a life of solitude.

Travis could see the headlines flashing in Kenton's eyes as he glanced at him throughout the evening. So far, he was honoring his sister's plea to leave him alone.

But they both knew it wouldn't last. Kenton Perkins was not one of the leading journalists in Jamaica for nothing.

After a large lunch that was mostly catered by Amelia's mother, there was a lull in the general conversation. Most of the men headed to the television where there was a rerun of a premier league match.

The women were engaged in a discussion about a Valentines Day dinner at Amelia's mother's church. They were currently arguing about doing away with the traditional red and white and using blue and green instead.

He wheeled to the end of the patio and looked over at the landscape. It was one of those exceptional days when it was not too chilly. The sun was out and golden, the skies blue and the breeze gentle. If he had functional legs, he would be taking a walk.

He needed an out from Amelia's place. He wasn't a football fan, neither did he think conversations about catering and decorating were particularly stimulating. He would rather be back at his apartment, listening to R&B oldies from the sixties and reading a paperback or talking to Skyler about her fanciful time travel idea.

Where did that thought come from? He had dismissed it earlier.

He looked at his palms and then curled them together. If only time travel was a reality, but it wasn't. He turned his wheelchair around. He had to find Amelia, tell her thank you for the meal but he had to go.

His eyes connected with Kenton's, who was sitting at the opposite end of the patio by himself. However, in no time he was standing in his path. For a big guy, Kenton moved pretty swiftly. He pulled up a chair, effectively blocking Travis from passing and then he laughed.

"I was testing a theory."

"What theory?" Travis locked the chair and sighed in defeat.

"The theory that if you look at a person hard enough, they will feel your stare and eventually look back at you."

"How did that work out for you?" Travis asked.

"You are remarkably indifferent to a person's stare." Kenton sniffed. "I promised not to hound you about your life for a story, that doesn't mean we can't have a conversation."

"Off the record." Travis raised an eyebrow.

"Yes. Sure." Kenton nodded. "I am an ethical person. Off the record is off the record."

Travis relaxed. "Your sister is coming to rescue me from you."

Amelia was bearing down on them with a scowl on her face.

"We are just talking." Kenton turned to Amelia.

"You sure he is not bothering you?" Amelia asked Travis and ignored her brother.

"Yes." Travis nodded. "I am fine. Thanks."

Amelia nodded and went back to the women.

"She is really into you," Kenton said. "You two are pretty serious, huh?"

Travis inhaled and then shook his head. "We are...were... just good friends."

"Good friends, really?" Kenton shook his head. "I never pegged Amelia as a girl who would date a guy in a wheelchair."

"I am a Jefferson, from the pharmaceutical Jefferson's." Travis twisted his mouth depreciatingly. "I am a good catch, crippled or not."

Kenton laughed. "You underestimate yourself, man. There is the fact that you have the movie star looks thing going on. I imagine that a couple of years ago you were a force to be reckoned with."

Travis shrugged. "I'd trade the looks for the legs."

"I imagine if I were in your position I would too." Kenton nodded, and then he grimaced. "Don't take this the wrong way but I've been curious about Winston Bayer, your friend, the one who crashed into you. How is he?"

Travis tensed. He hated to talk about Winston more than he hated to talk about his own experiences.

"He suffered a severe brain injury." Travis sighed. "His left side is unresponsive. He is bedridden. He cannot speak coherently."

Kenton whistled. "At the ripe old age of thirty-two, poor guy. You got off easy!"

"In a manner of speaking, yes." Travis gritted his teeth.

"Winston Bayer was a science prodigy wasn't he?" Kenton asked contemplatively, "He worked at Jefferson Pharmaceuticals in the scientific research department?"

"You know this already," Travis muttered.

"Yes." Kenton grimaced. "His mother blamed you for the accident, didn't she?"

Travis held up his hand. "Stop."

Kenton narrowed his eyes at Travis. "This is still so sensitive for you isn't it?"

"Obviously! I am in a wheelchair aren't I?" Travis snorted. "The accident was a sad occasion a decade ago that needs to be put to rest."

"But it's such an interesting story. Your accident and the murky details surrounding it," Kenton said contemplatively. "Anything about the mogul Miguel Jefferson is juicy news. His marriages, his children, his lifestyle are all fodder for speculation. There is nothing related to your father that will be put to rest."

Travis sighed. "Trust me. My father is not that interesting. He is just my dad. A man from humble beginnings who made a cough syrup that worked and built a business surrounding it."

"No," Kenton shrugged. "He is so much more. He is a businessman who was shrewd enough to know that one cough syrup was the tip of the iceberg. He was ruthless in business and ruthless in his love life."

Travis sighed. "This is all so dramatic."

"Why did you have such an antagonistic relationship with Winston Bayer?" Kenton asked, squinting his eyes and looking at Travis like they were in an interrogation room and his answer was vital to keeping him out of jail.

Travis chuckled dryly. "That is none of your business."

"Humor me," Kenton said grimly. "I am not going to be writing any of this. I just want to know. I have theories, but I want to hear your version."

Travis sighed. "I don't know why. We practically grew up together. His parents were close friends of the family. We went to the same schools, had the same friends, loved the same girls. When we met in the accident, we were fighting about Melanie Pitter."

"The supermodel?" Kenton widened his eyes, "she was the reason for your accident?"

"Yup." Travis nodded. "She loved the attention. We were both intimately involved with her. On the day of the accident we had found out that she was seeing both of us and in a stupid bid to impress Melanie had a water ski contest. Both of us were drunk.

"And now we are both disabled, and Melanie is happily married to my other friend, Duke Gillings, the only guy who was not drinking or partying or remotely interested in our competition for her."

"Irony." Kenton chuckled. "What irony! Isn't Duke the heir apparent to your father now?"

Travis scowled. "Yes, he is, only because I don't want the job."

"So Duke got the girl and will soon get the top job," Kenton said contemplatively. "And his mother, Arlene Gillings, wasn't she your housekeeper?"

"So?" Travis was curious to see where Kenton was going with this.

"Duke has a more than passing resemblance to Miguel Jefferson, especially around the eyes and mouth. Duke Gillings looks a lot more like your father than you do!"

"Get out of my way." Travis gritted out.

Kenton got up unhurriedly and moved the chair out of the way. "You never suspected did you?"

Travis wheeled past Kenton.

"Your father had a spare healthy son, just waiting to be dusted and polish and put in his place, a son that silently plotted to succeed him. That's why your father didn't make such a fuss when you decided to pursue academia."

Kenton continued walking beside him. "That's why he didn't even bother to reign you in when you were a wild playboy. He had his studious perfect son sitting at home, the one who didn't drink or party or had insane competitions with love rivals."

Travis stopped wheeling and looked at Kenton balefully. "You have no idea what you are talking about."

"Oh yes, I do," Kenton smirked. "I interviewed Duke Gillings a year ago as part of the paper's series on young businessmen under thirty. You know what I found out?"

"What?" Travis was curious despite the slow building anger that was pulsating in him.

"Duke Gillings is very much aware that he is the heir apparent. He speaks about your father as if he is a proud son and about you as if you deserve your injuries. It is not a coincidence that Duke is married to Melanie. It is not even a coincidence that you and Winston Bayer could never get along.

"I think Duke in his own quiet ruthless way directed his

life to exactly how it is right now. And he intended for you to be a casualty. He is happy that you are a cripple."

Travis couldn't speak after that last statement.

"Just thought that I would tell you," Kenton said a look of regret on his face. "I have always been meaning to say something. Sorry if I..."

"No, it's okay," Travis cleared his throat. "I need to go home."

He looked around. Amelia and the other ladies were nowhere to be seen, but he heard a cackle in the kitchen and then another. They were obviously in that area.

"Say my goodbyes will you."

"Sure." Kenton nodded and opened the front door for him. "I hope I didn't put my mouth where it didn't belong."

"No. It is fine. I have quite a bit to consider." Travis wheeled out of the house and into his car.

He drove out of the yard and then parked two blocks away. He had to process what Kenton had revealed to him.

Could any of it be true?

He covered his face with his hands and found that he could barely move from the position that he was in as reams and reams of memories about his past assailed him.

Memories with Duke always in the background, they were barely six months apart in age. In all of his memories, Duke was always around.

They had lived in the same house for twelve years until his mother had finally lobbied for Arlene Gillings to go. Travis had never understood the animosity his mom had felt towards Arlene.

Nor had he fully understood why his father had encouraged him to invite Duke along to whatever events they were going to together.

He had never had a solo outing with his dad while growing

up, Duke was always there.

Nor had he put any meaning to the long conversations that his dad would have with Arlene when he brought Duke back home. They often had heated secret discussions while he sat in the car and waited for his dad to come back to the car.

He had never questioned why his parent's former housekeeper, who had no job other than being a stay at home mom, could afford a house in an upper-class neighborhood, or how Duke could afford the private schools that he had attended, or how he could attend university without a scholarship or loans.

And he had never questioned why his father had bought him a car for his birthday and had done the same for Duke.

For the love of all that was holy, he was an idiot. Travis laughed harshly to himself. He had never thought to be suspicious of any of it. He had always thought his father was just generous to the housekeeper's son.

He smoked his first cigarette at seventeen because of Duke. Duke had encouraged him to do it.

He had tried marijuana because of Duke. Duke had rolled the blunt and given him to smoke. And sat and watched him and then asked him how it felt.

And drinking. Duke had shown up at his house with his little posse from the ghetto to celebrate with him, with two cases of beer.

He had missed several exams at college because of Duke. Duke had arranged parties for him at crucial times during his life. Pretending to be the good time friend while not participating in any of it.

It was clear Duke had wanted him to be drugged up, strung out and reckless.

It was also Duke who had suggested when they were around sixteen that Winston was jealous of him and he had swallowed the lie, treating Winston with suspicion, fighting with him over everything, turning their friendly rivalry into something sinister.

All along it had been Duke, the chief puppeteer, who was pulling his strings and now here he was the stupid crippled marionette living his life as far away from his parents as possible because he had thought that he had messed up and everyone was better off not seeing him every day.

His retreat had surely made it easy for Duke. He gritted his teeth in frustration, what could he do now?

Nothing, that's what. He had cut himself off from his father's business dashing the old man's hopes that he would carry on his legacy. He had deliberately pursued academia argued with his father that he couldn't handle running a large corporation as a cripple. At the time he had not been thinking clearly.

He was thinking now, and the bitter acid of regret spilled over in his stomach making him feel a very real urge to howl in frustration.

Chapter Seven

Something was wrong with Travis. Sky could tell. He seemed off. Maybe it was depression.

She watched him in class. He didn't smile with his eyes as he used to and he was less animated than he was at the beginning of the term.

At home, she was sure that something was off. His offer of friendship had never really taken off.

He was avoiding her. He wasn't even swimming in the mornings, and he had the song Dust In the Wind on repeat.

Hearing it through the patio doors was enough to depress her in the mornings. *I close my eyes only for a moment, and the moment's gone, all my dreams pass before my eyes, a curiosity, Dust in the wind, all they are is dust in the wind...* The song kept spinning in her head like a litany.

And to top it off, his midterm exams were almost cruel in their difficulty. It was as if he wanted the entire class to fail. He gave them questions about topics he hadn't even broached yet. It was a good thing that she had read ahead or else she would be groaning with the rest of the students in the exam room.

By Wednesday evening, her last day of exam, she was too tired to think much about it though. She had five whole days of Easter holidays to ponder the Travis Jefferson dilemma. She would sleep all day Thursday and then head home Friday.

She still needed to get that book about time travel and then she would come back the same evening. There was no need to linger; there was nothing for her to do at home and nobody to hang with.

She let herself into her apartment at the same time when she heard the other one, Travis' door opening.

She deliberately took her time and fumbled with the key, waiting until he appeared in her line of vision.

"Hey," he wheeled out on the corridor and looked at her contemplatively.

"Hello, Dr. Jefferson." She tucked a stray hair behind her ears and then dropped her hand self-consciously.

He grimaced. "It's a holiday, you are Skyler, and I am Travis. Deal?"

"Yes." she nodded eagerly.

"Why don't you come over for dinner?" Travis smiled. "I have Chinese takeout."

"Thank you." Sky grinned, "Dinner sounds good. I was going to eat leftover soup. I am just going to take a quick shower."

He went back inside and closed his door while she stood looking at the spot where he had been for longer than she had intended. She was now sure that there was something wrong with him. Behind his eyes had a hint of sadness that was not there before.

She hurried with her shower, pulling on comfortable

sweatpants and a red shirt.

By the time she pulled the comb through her hair and was on her way out, the phone rang.

"The food is getting cold." It was Travis.

She smiled. "I am on my way over."

She hung up the phone and hurried to the door.

****

"What are you doing for the holiday?" Travis had a plate of chow mein before him that he had barely touched. She had already gone through hers and was scarfing down a mound of rice and cashew chicken.

The Chinese restaurant on campus was exceptional.

"Nothing." She finished chewing her food and looked at him. "What are you doing?"

"The same. Nothing." His voice had an edge of despair to it.

Sky frowned. "Is everything okay with you?"

"No," Travis made a face. "And no I don't want to talk about it."

"Okay." Sky went back to her plate.

"I changed my mind," Travis muttered. "I do want to talk about it."

"You do?" Sky raised an eyebrow. She was acting nonchalant, but she wanted to know what was eating him. "I'll listen."

"A couple Sundays ago when I went to Amelia's..."

Sky snorted. "She is not that pretty, you know."

Travis paused and then started to laugh. "I beg to differ. She is very pretty, gorgeous even."

Sky clapped her hand over her mouth belatedly realizing

that she had sounded like a jealous toad.

Travis leaned forward in his chair and looked at her intently. "Being pretty can only take you so far..."

"I know. I do...I don't know why I said that" Sky said stricken, her voice cracking. "It was totally out of line."

Travis chuckled. "It is flattering that you are jealous, but Amelia and I are not a couple. I only went to her house to escape your friend Emma, and I think that it is a good thing I did. I had a conversation with Amelia's brother. He's a journalist who is fascinated with my family..."

Travis sighed and tapped his fingers on the edge of his chair. "And I learned things about my family that I was too blind to see. With one conversation he changed my whole world."

"Oh," Sky put down her fork. "What did he say?"

"That, I am not ready to talk about." Travis shrugged. "It's still so raw and fresh."

Sky sighed. "If it is that traumatizing for you why don't you go back and reset it?"

Travis laughed harshly. "I wish."

"You can do more than wish." Sky frowned at him. "You can change your life."

"That is such a tempting fantasy." Travis sighed. "If that were possible there are so many things I would not do."

"Like what?" Sky folded her arms under her chin and watched him. "Say this wasn't a fantasy, what would you do, where would you go back to?"

Travis chuckled. "Where? Summer 1986. I was twenty-one, just graduated college with my first degree, despite the odds. I was a wild guy in college and a very poor student. I probably graduated at the bottom of my class and only because my father was a big donor to the university."

Sky gasped, "Really? A boy version of Emma! How did

you get to be you now?"

"The accident that crippled me set me straight." Travis whistled. "I was in a coma for weeks. That helped with the detox. I was strung out on drugs that summer. I chain smoked marijuana, did some cocaine occasionally, drank beer like it was going out of style. Argued with my concerned mother and alienated my father. I was on a downward spiral that was alarming."

"So the accident was a good thing?" Sky wrinkled her brow contemplatively. "If you went back now and prevented the accident, you wouldn't be here now."

Travis nodded. "There is that. Maybe my parents would book me into one of those fancy drug rehab places, and I would be okay again."

"Or maybe I should go back to the time when I took my first drink or tried my first cigarette or maybe I should go back to the time when my housekeeper's son started to manipulate me silently."

"He did?" Sky stared at him unblinkingly. "Why?"

"Because he is my brother and he wanted me to fail so that he could take my place. I don't even know when he found out that we were related. The irony is that I thought he was my friend."

Sky realized that this was what he found out. This was what was eating him.

She didn't need to talk now Travis was going full flow. She watched as he ran his fingers through his wavy hair and as his deep brown eyes darkened in pain.

"I feel so stupid." He hung his head.

Sky shook her head. "No, you are not. You just didn't have foreknowledge. She went around to his side of the table and kneeled beside him.

"Hey, you know better than to beat up yourself about this.

Besides, you can change it. My cousin Addi was a resetter, and she changed our past. I made some decisions too that were beyond the pale, and she came back and fixed it for me. She changed things for our whole family."

Travis stared at her while she was speaking, no expression on his face. She stopped abruptly.

"What is it?"

"You are so pretty." He caressed her cheek and then his hands fell away. "Believe it or not, Sky, this resetter story is a nice distraction."

Sky got up and shook her head at him. "It's not a story."

She started clearing the table. "Where do you keep your containers for leftovers?"

Travis shook his head. "I don't eat leftovers. You can dump it."

"My mother would be horrified." Sky smirked at him. "I eat leftovers. I am taking this next door."

Travis nodded. "Okay, *bon appétit.*"

She scraped the food together and put them in a ceramic dish. While she did this, she could feel the imprint of his fingers where he had caressed her face.

She snuck a peek at him while she was packing the food and he was staring blankly at the wall. She wanted him to take her seriously. She wanted to help him, but what could she do?

How could she make him believe?

"I am going home tomorrow," She said out loud. «Want to come?"

Travis turned around and smiled. "We had one meal together, and you are asking me to meet the parents?"

Sky chuckled. "No, just going to collect a book. You might meet the parents because I have to say hi to them but..."

He looked like he was going to say no.

"I'll drive," Sky said before he could vocalize his refusal. "Your wheelchair can hold in the back of the car."

He opened his mouth to reply, and Sky said hurriedly. "It's better than staying here and playing Dust In the Wind."

Travis grinned. "You have a point. I'll come with you. Want to watch a movie?"

"Depends." Sky grinned. "If you are into stuff that will depress me for days I'm not interested."

"Relax," Travis wheeled toward the living room. "The guy at the video rental shop said it was the most rented movie he had. I am sure it wouldn't make you cry."

Chapter Eight

They left out at ten the next morning. Sky was yawning so wide that she heard her jawbones crack.

Travis laughed at her. "You're sure you're up to this? Your eyes are still red and puffy from all the crying you did last night. The Lion King really did you in. I thought everybody had watched it but me. When it was released in '94, it was all the rage."

"I am sure I am up to driving, and we didn't have a VCR when it was released in '94." Sky massaged her face and then started the car. "Don't act so flippant. I saw your eyes glinting when Scar murdered Mufassa. You were going to cry."

Travis chuckled. "Nope, I wasn't. I felt a twinge, but I remained stoic throughout the whole show. It was a cartoon for crying out loud!"

"I think I am going to name my son, Simba and my daughter Nala," Sky said grinning. "It had that much of an impact on me."

Travis laughed and adjusted his dark glasses over his eyes. He looked relaxed today, much better than he had been looking in the weeks before.

"You comfy?" Sky asked as she slowed down over a particularly large pothole.

"Yep." Travis nodded. "Why wouldn't I be?"

"I don't know anything about your disability," Sky said carefully. "I have never seen you drive in anything but your van."

He turned to look at her. "What do you want to know about my disability?"

Sky flushed. She could feel her ears getting warm. What she wanted to know would take only the boldness of Emma and the kind of frankness that she would never develop in a million years. She went for the safe questions, the light ones. "I don't know. How bad is it? What happened?"

"Accident on a jet ski," Travis murmured. "I was racing a buddy of mine in Ocho Rios. We collided."

"Yikes." Sky glanced at him.

"We were both knocked unconscious. When I woke up, I couldn't feel my legs. When he woke up, he couldn't talk or remember names or feel his right side."

"Wow." Sky looked at his legs and then back at the road.

"Next burning question," Travis said softly.

She swallowed. This was her chance, but she chickened out. "Er, I...what's it like to be in a wheelchair?"

Travis grinned. Sky had a funny feeling that he was on to her. He answered the question dutifully.

"Everything takes longer to get done. You can't just get up and walk to wherever or jump out of bed or use the bathroom quickly. It sucked at first, but I passed the self-pity stage ages ago.

"After I reached my fifth anniversary I accepted the situation. Walking was not going to happen for me again, so I just had to live with who I was now."

"You gave up hope?"

"Nah, I became realistic. I did my masters and then the doctorate and started teaching. I focused my energies on something other than my disability. I learned to get around. I learned to live on my own. I accepted that life went on. Not to say that sometimes I don't feel nostalgic about using my legs again. Sometimes I dream that I am running and I wake up happy. Next question."

Sky nodded. "I wanted to ask about..."

"Restrooms?" Travis raised an eyebrow. "They can be a pain if the stalls are too narrow. I am very grateful for Mount Faith's restrooms for the disabled. I think as a country we do not cater for people with mobility problems. We have tiny bathrooms and too many stairs."

"Oh," Sky bit her lip. "It never crossed my mind about how you er maneuvered yourself into and out of restrooms."

"So what crossed your mind?" Travis asked, a lock of hair fell over his shades; he looked like a movie star.

"Nothing, my curiosity is cured," Sky said feeling self-conscious.

"Sex." Travis chuckled. "You left out the most obvious topic. Your friend Emma asked me about that the first day she came trotting by the pool."

Sky sputtered. "She did?"

"Yup." Travis grinned. "Now, admit you were curious."

"I was curious. I was dying with it. Emma kept telling me about sex in wheelchairs and all of that jazz. And I am officially mortified."

"I know this was a curiosity for you," Travis smirked. "Your stammering and blushing gave you away. What do you want to know about it?"

Sky groaned. "This is embarrassing."

"I would be curious too." Travis grinned.

He didn't say anything more after that. Sky was squirming in her seat in suspense.

Travis touched her leg briefly, and she jumped.

"Relax," he pushed his glasses further on his head so that she could see his eyes. "When you are no longer my student, maybe we'll talk about it. Maybe not. But to give you a general answer, some people in wheelchairs can have sex and can father children. "Being disabled gives you a sense of vulnerability, giving details about your sex life especially to pretty, young students is not something I want to do unless I trust you."

Sky swallowed. "That's fair."

"Tell me about your family." Travis changed the subject.

"We are not as exciting as yours." Sky shrugged. "I told you about them already. My mom is Mrs. Bucket from Keeping Up Appearances, remember that British Comedy? They shouldn't have canceled it when they did."

"Yes I remember it, I am just now watching the reruns." Travis laughed, "You serious? Your mother is Hyacinth Bucket?"

"Well, she is a little like her. Everything has to be just right for my mother. She is a bit OCD about a lot of things." Sky chuckled. "On the other hand, my dad is a regular guy who drinks beer, watches an obscene amount of sporting events and is not afraid to bet on them. He is jovial, sweet and takes everything at face value. He is not particularly deep."

"He sounds like a nice guy to hang with," Travis glanced at her, "and the polar opposite of my dad."

"What's your dad like?" Sky asked turning at a crossroad. She honked her horn at a group of children who were playing cricket in the middle of the street.

Travis watched as they scampered for the safety of the side of the road before he answered.

"My dad is a businessman. He is intense and overly analytical. Everything has to have an explanation, or he will drive himself crazy trying to get to the bottom of it. He was a science nerd in the seventies, a businessman in the eighties.

"He excelled at both. He did make an effort to be a good role model when I was younger, and now he hates the fact that I am crippled. He can't handle anything less than perfect, so our relationship is pretty non-existent now."

"And your mom?" Sky asked, "What is she like?"

"My mom is a nurturer," Travis chuckled, "with a magical green thumb that can bring any plant back to life."

Sky laughed. "Come on, really? Any plant."

"Yes, My mom's a botanist and a true plant lover." Travis smiled, "I think I learned the scientific names for plants before I learned their common names."

"Cool." Sky looked at him with envy. "That's cool and unusual."

Travis nodded. "Well, I was teased for it in high school. When you know information like what we call grass from the Poaceae family which includes edible grass like rice, wheat, and barley, you tend to be looked at like a know it all."

Sky chuckled. "Yes, I can see how that would happen. How did your parents meet?"

"My dad went to Trinidad to see her about a plant she was studying. She wrote a science journal article about its use to cure certain strains of influenza.

My father was studying the same plant for his now famous cough medicine. And as they say, the rest was history. They hit it off instantly. They didn't waste any time. They married within a month. Five miscarriages later they had me."

"Wow." Sky glanced at him, "so you are a momma's boy."

"Surprisingly, my mother is not that clingy. We have a healthy relationship." Travis laughed. "She has a lot to occupy her outside of my life. She keeps tabs on the research section of the business, and she owns a garden center."

"That's where you got your pretty plants from?" Sky raised an eyebrow.

"Definitely." Travis nodded.

"Tell me about your dad's first wife. Do you get along with her?"

"Marla, I hardly see her. She remarried twice after my dad. She is now single, I think. My sister, Milly, who is closest to me in age is usually the one who keeps me up to date on her mom, but Milly is in no frame of mind to give me family suss now..."

Sky was going to ask about Milly, but she had a feeling that this would not be something he was willing to elaborate on, so instead, she asked, "How did they break up? Your dad and Marla?"

Travis sighed. "They were teenage lovers. They had a shotgun marriage and three children later, they both couldn't stand each other and Marla left. My dad noticed she was gone a couple of weeks after she left, thus making her point that she was superfluous to his life."

"Weeks?" Sky squealed. "You have to be kidding!"

"No." Travis chuckled, "Marla and my dad tell the same version of the story."

Sky whistled.

"How did your parents break up?" Travis asked curiously.

Sky sighed. "They cheated on each other. My mother was going to pay her lover to kill him. My cousin Addi time traveled back to '92 and foiled the plan. So that's why my dad is alive and remarried to Monica."

"Good old time travel, huh?" Travis glanced at her doubtfully. "You look so sane when you tell me these things."

"That's because I am sane," Sky said after a long contemplative silence. "One day you will believe me. One day you will get desperate enough to try resetting as a solution. When you do, you have to find me and tell me about it."

Travis laughed out loud. "Never."

"You know what they say," Sky shook her head at him reprovingly, "never say never. You just never know."

****

Sky debated whether she should drive up to Monica's place before she got the book; she slowed down in front of her house and looked over into the yard. Her uncle and aunt were not at their house. She had a key though so getting the book from Addi's room would not be a problem.

The flowers at the front of her house were wilting, and her father would not have the intuition to water them. Besides that, the place had an air of neglect to it that suggested that nobody was living there.

"That's where you live?" Travis looked over into the yard curiously.

"Yes, I think that should be lived, past tense. My childhood stuff is taking up space. My dad lives up there."

She pointed to the house on the hill.

Travis whistled. "Nice view and nice flowers on the hill. I can see why he moved up there."

"Yes." Sky smirked. "It is a nice place. Monica said the name of the flowers in the driveway are Yesterday Today and Tomorrow."

"Or brunfelsia pauciflora," Travis said smugly.

"The problem with you telling me this is that I have no idea if what you are saying is even right. I am just going to nod and pretend that I am impressed."

Travis laughed.

"Monica says her grandmother planted them like twenty odd years ago. She liked them because the flowers represented very distinct periods in our timeline. The first day they are purple (yesterday), the second day they change to a pastel lavender shade (today), and on the third day, they change to an almost white color (tomorrow). You can just look at the plant and see where each flower is. I guess the whole time thing resonated with Miss Gwen because she was a time traveler."

"Good heavens." Travis covered his face. "Everybody in your life is a time traveler."

"I never met Miss Gwen." Sky shrugged. "Probably I did and was too young to remember. She was not in my life, though. She was my stepmother's grandmother. I wish you would stop mocking the resetting idea."

"Okay, okay." Travis looked at her lazily. "I will not say a word against your little time traveling theory again."

"Good." Sky tapped the steering wheel. "I guess I should drive on up there and say hi. It would look bad for me not to."

Travis touched her on the arm. "Your dad would like that."

"Maybe," Sky muttered. She took a deep breath and started the car. She drove up to the steep driveway and turned off the engine.

As if on cue, the door was flung open, and Monica walked out. She was an attractive woman in her late thirties. Her son was attached to her hip, his head on her shoulders.

Sky got out of the car and dredged up a smile. She didn't

dislike Monica. She just didn't like the fact that she was no longer the center of her father's world and had to share him with Monica and Michael.

"Look, it's your sister Skyler," Monica was saying to the cute chubby toddler.

Sky went closer to the veranda. "I am just passing through, thought I'd say hi."

"Just passing through?" Monica frowned, "Oh Skyler, we would love your company, you know. I thought you'd spend half term with us."

And then Monica looked beyond Sky and into the car, and she stopped her protests. "You have a friend along. Why don't you join us inside? Your father is in the shower. I could rustle up some brunch."

"No thanks, I am full." Sky looked around at Travis hoping he'd say he was full too and they could just get on their way.

"I wouldn't mind coming in." Travis smiled at Monica, "Sky could you help me out? My wheelchair?"

Traitorous Travis. Sky glanced at his smiling face with a scowl.

"Sure," Sky said out loud because Monica was watching.

"This is a brief visit," Sky whispered fiercely after retrieving the wheelchair from the back. "Brief!"

"Fine," Travis whispered back.

Sky helped him into the chair and straightened up and walked beside him toward the veranda, making the introductions and watching as Monica tried to cover up her shock at seeing that Travis was in a wheelchair. She was quite good at it too—pulling chairs out of the way and making way for him on the veranda with a pleasant expression on her face.

Michael wanted to get out of her hand and inspect the wheeling chair closer, but she was hanging on to him for dear life.

Sky decided to intervene. She hadn't seen the little tyke for weeks now, and she had to admit that a secret part of her did like him.

She held out her hands for him, and he hugged her around the neck.

"Sky! Sky!" He squealed it quite close to her ears; she winced and had to hold on to him tightly as he reached down for Travis. "Dada"

"Not Dada," Sky chuckled. "Travis."

Walking to the far end of the veranda with him. He started to cry so she handed him to Monica who put him down on the ground, and he walked straight over to Travis and held his hands up.

"Good Lord," Sky laughed. "I am not interesting around here anymore."

Travis picked him up and moved the chair around with him, and Michael chortled with glee.

Sky sat down and shook her head. "Traitor."

Monica laughed. "So how are you, Sky?"

"Good," Sky said tiredly. "I am passing all of my subjects this semester. "

"I am looking forward to spending some time with you in the summer," Monica said gently.

"Not going to happen. I am hoping to pick up a job for the first summer session. I have to pay for my second summer session out of pocket. That was the agreement with dad."

Travis looked over at her when she said that and then continued rocking along with a giggling Michael.

Monica looked disappointed. "Stan and I were thinking that we could have a family vacation in the summer, maybe spend two weeks at Disney World."

"Disney World! Sounds like fun but I am almost sure that

my summer will be too busy."

"Such a shame." Monica looked disappointed; Sky could tell that she was working hard to include her in their family unit. Maybe she should stop considering herself an outsider and at least meet Monica halfway.

"I might come home the week after exams and stay here instead if I don't get a job immediately."

"That would be great!" Monica smiled widely. "Very good."

"What's very good?" Stan came to the door, smelling minty from his aftershave.

Sky jumped up and ran to greet him. "Daddy!"

"Sky love." Stan was grinning from ear to ear as he hugged his daughter. Picking her up in the air and swinging her around. Both of them uncaring that they had an audience; they made it pretty plain that they were happy to see each other.

Monica and Travis looked at their long greeting and smiled.

"So who is this?" Stan finally asked as he put Sky back down on the ground.

"My friend and neighbor Travis," Sky said quickly. "Somehow she didn't think to introduce him as her lecturer would be cool with her father. It would create too many questions. Like how old was he and what were his intentions, and all of those awkward things that she did not want to address right now.

"Travis this is my dad, Stanley Porter."

"Or just Stan." Her father held out his hand to be shaken, and Travis took it.

Monica gasped.

Travis looked at Monica. "Is something wrong?"

"No," Monica shook her head, "not at all, it's just that you have two lines in your palms. It's pretty rare."

"I told him about it already, Monica," Sky sighed, "but he doesn't believe me."

"So this resetter myth is believed by your whole family?"

Sky chuckled and shook her head.

Stan shrugged. "It's true. My niece Addi was a resetter. She gave me some nice bets a couple of years ago when she came back from the future. Monica's granny was a resetter who never acted on it. So hey, why not believe?"

Travis nodded doubtfully. He probably thought that they had all lost their minds.

****

"That's the blue rock." Sky drove as close to the stone as she could manage after the long visit with Monica and her dad. She had found the book in the first drawer of Addi's desk and had given it to Travis. He was looking at the book and then the stone, an incredulous expression on his face.

"Why is the rock blue?"

"I don't know," Sky shrugged. "Some geologist came by to look at it a couple of years ago and said it had azurite and quartz and something else in it. He said it was nothing that we could sell for loads of cash, so we left it alone."

Travis nodded and then grinned. "So how would this work? I place my special palms on the rock and then voila I am thrown back in time."

"No." Sky rolled her eyes at him. She got out of the car and placed her palms in the groove, shaped like a palm and demonstrated, you place your palm here.

You think about the year you want to go back to and if you are taking back anything with you. You have to make sure that it was available in the time that you were going back to, and you have to clutch it in your other palm and place it on the rock too."

"Sounds quite simple." Travis grinned. The rain started to drizzle, and Travis gestured for her to get back in the car.

Sky returned to the car with a huff. "I wish Monica had impressed upon you how serious this is."

Travis held up his palms and looked at them. "It's weird. You know I have never had anybody point out that my palms were unusual before I met you and your kooky family."

Sky chuckled. "Max Ehrman's Desiderata has a part of a line that says, listen to others, even to the dull and the ignorant; they too have their story."

"Ah, okay, I guess I can't disobey the desiderata." Travis curled his hand into a fist. He fell silent.

Sky glanced at him. "Maybe you should first read the book. It's Monica's grandmother's diary, and then I'll tell you about my cousin, Addi and what she did."

"Fine. I'll read it," Travis said then added. "Someday."

Sky shook her head in despair. "I don't understand you. If I heard that I had the chance to reset my life I would jump at it."

"Why? You are just nineteen; you haven't yet done anything to feel regretful about."

"You have a point." Sky watched the rain rivulets on the windscreen. "My cousin has already changed things for me."

"What do you mean?" Travis asked.

"I don't want to talk about it now." Sky sighed. "I still feel stupid when I think about what I would have done if she hadn't changed the course of my life."

Travis whistled. "Fascinating. My guess is it involved a guy."

"Yes." Sky glanced at him. "Good guess."

"When I was your age, it was a girl, Melanie. The reason I am in this wheelchair. Well, that and stupidity. I was mad at a friend who was also seeing her."

Sky felt a shaft of jealousy that was quite apparent in her voice when she finally asked, "You still like her?"

"No, not like I did when we were younger," Travis said. "She heard that I would be in a wheelchair and she bolted. I don't blame her. What nineteen-year-old girl in her right mind would enjoy hanging with a handicapped man? Women want vitality and a show of strength. They love alpha males, guys who can defend them from things that go bump in the night."

Sky laughed uncomfortably. She was feeling the opposite of those things toward him. "Not all women are like that."

She was not like that. She was fighting a humongous crush that was on the verge of stifling her.

"Most of them are," Travis shrugged. "It is nothing to be ashamed of. It's human nature. An instinct to keep the planet populated with the best of the species, the survival of the fittest and all of that. Defective males are not as valued because well... they are defective."

Sky turned to him fully. "I am not like that."

Travis turned his head and looked at her languidly. "Why not? Why do you like a thirty-one-year-old cripple?"

"I..." Sky swallowed.

Travis put a finger on her lips. "I have nothing to offer you. I am not going to get better miraculously. I will not walk again. I am only good for a two-minute crush. You'll soon wise up and move on."

"How can you say that?" Sky groaned as he took the pad of his fingers and moved it against her lips almost absently.

He removed his hand and she could breathe normally again.

He was still looking at her, and she didn't want him to see that just his finger on her lips had her inside shaking like an earthquake.

She bit her lip.

"Come here," Travis whispered hoarsely. She leaned toward him close, too close, their noses touched.

She could feel his breath.

He fished one hand in her hair and held her steadily while he stared into her eyes. "We shouldn't be doing this."

Sky could hear her heart thudding in her ears. She had never anticipated anything as much as she was anticipating this kiss.

Somebody moaned.

Maybe it was him or maybe her? He pulled her closer until they were lip to lip. She was breathing him in. His lips parted hers and then her arms were around his neck, and she was kissing him back as hungrily as he was kissing her.

Travis was the first to pull away. He looked into her eyes deeply and seriously, "Sky, this should never have happened. I am still your lecturer. This is highly inappropriate."

Sky nodded, feeling a little light headed. Now, that was what a kiss was supposed to be.

"Are you listening to me, Sky?" Travis' voice was husky.

Sky nodded as soon as the roar in her ears died down. "Sure. I am...listening."

She straightened her top that had ridden up on her belly and started the car.

Travis touched her arm. "You okay?"

"Fine." Sky nodded jerkily. "Just fine."

Chapter Nine

Travis was sitting in his office alone near the end of April when Amelia walked in.

"What's going on?" She flung down the daily newspaper on his desk and folded her arms crossly.

"What?" Travis looked up from the computer where he was fine-tuning exam questions which were required by the department chair by the end of the day. He was behind schedule.

"Your father's super exclusive birthday bash." Amelia closed the office door and sat down. "I thought you would have invited me as your plus one."

"I didn't remember about it."

Travis glanced at the headline: *Miguel Jefferson celebrates 70 in June. Will be announcing his replacement as head of Jefferson Pharmaceuticals.*

"But that's crazy!" Amelia squinted at him and then said, accusation heavy in her voice, "That means the rumors are true!"

Travis had his hands poised to type a full stop. Instead, he looked up at her and frowned. "What rumors?"

"The one about you dating your student." Amelia frowned. "I was inclined to believe it at first because you have been very aloof this past month."

Six weeks. Travis corrected her in his head. Six weeks, where he spent an obscene amount of time with Skyler Porter. After that scorching kiss at her childhood home, they had tried to pretend that it hadn't happen, but the pretence had only lasted for a week, after that, Sky came over to his place regularly. They cooked together. Well, she cooked he watched.

They watched movies together. He read while she studied. She swam with him in the mornings. She nagged him to read the diary, and he kept putting it off. They talked a lot about everything.

Sky found him fascinating. She craved being with him. And he was not unaffected. He was addicted to her. That was the only way he knew to describe the unfamiliar emotions assailing him.

It was new and frightening, and he knew it wouldn't last. It couldn't. He should have put a stop to it from that kiss.

Amelia glared at him as he sank deeper in silence.

"It can't be true!" Amelia hissed. "You know that dating students is against the rules!"

Travis sighed. "She won't be my student for much longer. Exams are twelve days away."

Amelia gasped, her mouth hanging open inelegantly. "Travis, you know better than this."

"I do." Travis nodded, "now please can we talk about something else?"

"No!" Amelia huffed, "we had a thing."

"Had." Travis curved his fingers under his chin and stared at Amelia frankly. "I now have someone in my life who likes me for me. Not because I am related to the Jefferson's. It is a heady feeling."

"This is ridiculous, Travis. I like you, I always have."

Travis snorted. "You started speaking to me after you found out that I was one of the Jefferson's from Jefferson Pharmaceutical."

"That's not true." Amelia protested weakly and then changed tactics. "Who is to say that this girl, what's her name, isn't with you for the grade?"

Travis laughed. "She is not."

"I am morally obligated to report this to the university president." Amelia stood up stiffly.

"What exactly are you going to say?" Travis asked unconcerned and then raised an eyebrow. "You know what? Don't tell me, I am looking forward to the phone call from Edwards."

Amelia paused at the door. "You can be intimate with a woman, can't you?"

Travis looked at her incredulously. "You ask me that now? When you took great pains to skirt that issue when you were feigning an interest in me."

Amelia looked contrite. "I had doubts about being with you. It is a huge responsibility being with a crippled man and that's why I am almost sure that this girl is playing with you. Crippled men are not a girl's first choice. Believe it or not, in all of this, I am most concerned about you."

Travis winced through her little self-righteous speech. He had more or less said the same thing to Sky.

He waved off Amelia so-called concern and turned back to his computer. He hoped that she got the message.

She did.

She left his office soon after.

He sat back in his chair and looked up into the ceiling. He hadn't been this happy since he was...He couldn't remember being this happy.

It was strange. He had reached the ripe old age of thirty-one and couldn't pinpoint a time when he rushed out of bed, eager to face the day, when he could see her face or hear her laughter or just watch as she spoke.

It had all happened so fast, at least for him. It had taken him a year to warm to Amelia, with Sky a few weeks. To be honest when he had first seen Sky he had been more than mildly interested.

The internal phone rang jerking him out of his self-assessment.

"Hello dear," his mother said when he answered. "How are you?"

"I am good mom." Travis smiled. His mother's voice was always a welcomed addition to his day. This was the voice that had brought him back from the brink of despair when he woke up in the hospital ten years ago.

"How are you?" He asked.

"The family is in a bit of an uproar at the moment." She paused. "I shouldn't bother you with this."

"Bother me," Travis insisted. "My legs are not working but I can assure you my ears are."

She chuckled at that. But it was a forlorn sound. Almost forced.

"Can you come home for the summer or are you doing classes?"

Travis considered her loaded question. His mother never pressed him to come home; she had supported him moving from Kingston and taking up academia. This was the first time since the accident that she was asking him to return home.

Her voice sounded a little desperate.

"What's going on, Mom? What is the family uproar?"

His mother sighed. "Didn't Carly or Beth call you?"

His sisters. He was not that close to them. They spoke at family gatherings. Carly was a banker; her husband sat on the board at Jefferson Pharmaceuticals, his sister Elizabeth, co-owned a funeral home. Her three sons worked at the company in various managerial positions.

His youngest sister, Milly, the sister closest to his age, was a drug addict who had more or less lived in and out of rehab for the last ten years and he had arranged for her to stay at his Kingston apartment for the past three months.

"No." Travis frowned. "What's going on?"

"Your father has gone crazy." His mother's voice became husky with despair. "He is going to make Duke Gillings the head of the company! That is not going to happen not over my dead body. Never!"

Travis sighed. He had tried to forget that revelation by Kenton, that Duke was his brother. Maybe if he was close to his dad, he could have asked him about it.

"Mom," Travis felt a sharp pain in his heart, "Duke is his son."

"I don't care." Pasha gritted out plainly. "This business is around today because my father bailed Miguel out of the financial mess he was in. I have the same amount of shares that Miguel does." Pasha was breathing hard. "I am not going to stand by and watch as this business is taken over by Arlene Gillings' son!

"He is smug, entitled, and downright dangerous and if nobody else sees it, I do. I am going to put a stop to this now. I need your help."

Travis gasped. "I had no idea that..."

"Because you detached yourself from the business!" Pasha snapped. "You gave that immoral creep, Duke Gillings a foothold into our company. Your father is planning to announce his succession plan to the world on his birthday.

"And I guess he is going to confess that Duke is his and then they are going to change his name and hand him our company on a platter."

Travis inhaled. "Mom, when did you find out about Duke?"

"I always knew that Arlene was a threat," Pasha growled. "She was at the house before I got married to your father, playing wife. I guess they thought they could continue after I got here.

"Some things you don't want to face. If I had acknowledged that I knew that Duke was his, I could have cut off the head of the monster before it began and they wouldn't have felt the need to go behind my back and strike deals and make insane decisions!"

"But Mom," Travis swallowed, "if I come home this summer, what am I going to do to change Dad's mind?"

"He will remember that he has another son." Pasha sighed. "He will know that just because you are in a wheelchair doesn't mean that you are invisible! Just come home. I have a plan and a thirty percent stake in Jefferson Pharmaceuticals. Your father has to respect that kind of power."

Travis hung up the phone feeling disturbed.

****

Sky was on her way to Travis' office when she saw Amelia Perkins marching towards the door. She made a detour to the cafeteria instead. The last thing she wanted was to go to the office with Amelia Perkins looking at her suspiciously. She had Amelia for the second summer session, Macro

Economics. She had just signed up; it was as good as done.

Now she needed to find an eight-week job that could pay for the four courses she had just signed up for.

Most of the on-campus jobs were long taken. She slowed down at the entrance to the cafeteria to check the notice board anyway.

Most of the notices were for summer rentals.

"I would think that since you are seeing Doctor Hotty you could just sit out the summer," Emma said behind her, "or at least get a spot on his company's industrial placement scheme."

Sky spun around. Emma had a headphone around her neck, and a Walkman clipped to her jeans pocket and was looking considerably slimmer.

"Hi." Sky tried not to act too shocked. She hadn't seen Emma in class for weeks.

"You can say it," Emma muttered, "I look like hell warmed up, chewed up and spit out."

"No," Sky shook her head, "not really. You've lost a ton of weight though. Where've you been?"

"In Fluville," Emma muttered. "You are so caught up in your little romance with the man in wheelchair you didn't realize I was missing, did you?"

"I noticed. I thought you were doing your usual, class skipping."

"Nah." Emma cleared her throat. "I had the flu then got pneumonia. Did a one-week stay in the hospital. They injected me like four times a day. I think my butt has holes in it."

Sky headed to the food section with Emma walking behind her. Emma only chose a fruit plate and water. Sky chose the same; she was still full from breakfast.

"Why did you say I had a romance with Dr. Jefferson?"

Sky asked as soon as they sat down. She couldn't wait until they were out of earshot to accost Emma about it.

"People said they see you two together and you looked chummy," Emma said biting into a mango slice.

"I don't have an appetite." She looked at the fruit plate dispassionately. "I still feel like I am readjusting."

Sky inhaled. "I wish people would mind their own business."

Emma looked at her and then laughed. "Really? If we minded our own business, the world would be so dull and friendless and colorless. We need to be our brother's keeper; no man is an island...yadda... yadda."

"Got it." Sky smirked.

"You two did the deed yet?" Emma sipped some water and looked at Sky slyly. "You can tell me. I won't tell a soul."

Sky chuckled. "I know you wouldn't tell a soul; you would tell several souls."

"I am not a gossip," Emma protested unconvincingly. "I am just your garden variety friendly non-judgmental ear."

Sky chuckled. "I am not going to talk about that."

"Why not?" Emma wheedled. "There is nothing else juicy to talk about unless you had a catfight with Amelia Perkins, or he is bringing you to meet the parents. Is he?"

"No." Sky sighed. "Here is something juicy to discuss, exam is in a couple of days."

"You should insist on meeting the parents." Emma ignored her, "I heard that they live in a mansion in the St Andrew hills with a garden that is out of this world. The mother is a botanist or something..."

Sky rolled her eyes. "I am not engaging you till you change the topic."

"Industrial Placement Scheme," Emma said smugly, "Jefferson Pharmaceuticals hires university students every summer. I signed up. My parents are playing hardball said I had to work for the summer because I wasted my time last year."

Sky raised an eyebrow. "I would do that. Unfortunately, I don't know anyone in Kingston."

"You know me!" Emma said excitedly, "And what's more, we have room in the castle for you. My parents are excellent hosts."

"No thanks." Sky shook her head.

"Don't dismiss it, unless you are going to be staying with your boyfriend?" Emma was back to being nosy.

"He is not..." Sky paused. What were they really? They had become extremely close in the past couple of weeks.

She spent more time in his apartment than hers. Maybe they were close friends who once shared a kiss. A kiss she could still remember in stark detail. A kiss that she brought to life in her mind before going to sleep, before she showered, in the middle of class when he was speaking, and at odd times during her study group...

"Oh Sky," Emma snapped her fingers before her eyes. "You are staring into space."

"Sorry." Sky cleared her throat. "As I said, Dr. Jefferson is just a friend and neighbor."

Emma speared a fruit and then grinned. "I so believe you."

And then Emma miraculously changed the subject. "Want to help me with an overdue project?"

"No." Sky shook her head, "I have eight exams to study for."

"I'll give you my cassette," Emma held up her Walkman. "I have Celine Dion, Mariah Carey, Tony Rich Project on here. Weren't you crazy about that song, Nobody Knows it But Me, earlier this year?"

Sky looked at the cassette and pretended to consider the

offer.

"No thanks, I would help you only if you had the Waiting To Exhale CD," Sky scratched her chin, "but then again, my cousin Addi said she'd send it to me next month."

She got up and closed her fruit plate. "Take care, Emma."

Chapter Ten

"**Y**ou are exceptionally quiet tonight," Travis said in the silence. Sky had entered the apartment earlier with a stack of books and past papers and had made her way to his couch, turned on the radio to Rick Dees weekly top 40 charts and had effectively ignored him.

Not even Return of the Mack, a song she usually went crazy over, could stir her from her intense concentration.

Sky looked over at him and frowned. "Sorry. What time is it?"

"Time for you to take a break from studying," Travis wheeled closer to her and looked into her eyes. "You are tired. You should rest."

He pointed at her mounds of papers covering his settee. "Close your eyes, relax."

"Easy for you to say." Sky rubbed the back of her neck. "You are not the student."

"I was a student once," Travis murmured, "and I have

found that relaxing between bouts of studying worked."

"Maybe." Sky leaned back in the settee and put her heavy textbook beside her with a sigh. "I saw Emma today."

Travis chuckled. "Me too. She had her doctor's letter and meticulously explained why she wasn't around. She mentioned working at Jefferson Pharmaceuticals this summer too. She threatened me to put in a good word with the HR department in forceful Emma style."

Sky grimaced. "I would ask you to do the same for me, but I have nowhere to stay in Kingston, and I would never want to stay with Emma. One semester of living with her has cured me."

"You could stay at my apartment," Travis offered lightly. "It has three bedrooms. My sister Milly lives there now, so you can get the guest room. It's also walking distance from the head office. You could work in the president's office. My dad's admin assistant, Betty, always needs an assistant. It would be an invaluable experience for you. You could get to see the inner running of the place."

Sky sat up straighter. "You are kidding!"

"No. I am not." Travis shrugged. "I can call the relevant people tomorrow."

"Thank you, Travis." Sky whispered. "Thank you."

"You are welcome. It's selfish of me. I don't want to miss you this summer since I have to be in Kingston as well. There is a bit of a power play going on at the office, and my mother wants me to be around and flex my muscles."

Sky widened her eyes and looked at him a coy smile playing around her lips. "You'd miss me?"

Travis nodded. "Yes."

"So would you categorize us as... er... more than friends?"

Travis backed away from her. "No talk about any of this until you are officially not my student.

Sky chuckled and picked up the book she was absorbed in earlier. "Counting the days, Dr. Jefferson."

****

Travis couldn't sleep after Sky left. His sister Milly called him pretty late to complain about his housekeeper, June who was watching her suspiciously.

Travis soothed her somewhat and hung up the phone, making a mental note to call June and ask her to back off a bit. Milly was staying at his apartment for a month because she had nowhere else to go.

She had shafted everyone who had helped her in the past somehow. All family members were on high alert even Milly's mother Marla.

Milly had stolen from Marla time and time again to feed her habit. Travis hoped she would kick her addiction for good this time around.

He dearly hoped so.

It pained his heart to think about it. Milly was just five years older than he was; she had been battling addiction for over half of her life.

He turned on the lamp. He didn't want to think about his family right now.

He didn't want to think.

He should probably lose himself in a book and then hopefully fall asleep, but he had no books close by other than that diary that Sky had insisted that he read.

He picked it up reluctantly. On the very first page was the title: *Resetters And Their Special Gift.*

"I am really reading this," he muttered to himself and skipped to the next page and began reading.

This diary was written June 3, 1975

My name is Gwendolyn Fisher Campbell, and I am a resetter. I know I have the gift to reset events, but I won't go back. Even though Vernon is not here with me anymore. I will not take the chance. What if I go back and I change something? Will my family change?

I couldn't bear that. I would love to set some of my life events the way I think would be ideal but the past for me should be firmly left where it belongs, in the past.

I met a resetter once; his name was Oswald King, the writer of the article attached to this book.

He was born in 1889, and he had the gift to reset. I sought him out after reading the article attached in 1949, by that time he was sixty years old and living as a recluse in the hills of St. Andrew. He sent regular articles to the Daily Paper mostly surrounding the things that he changed in the past.

He called his articles How It Was Before.

Of course, nobody took his stories literally, it was to them a good piece of alternative historical fiction. A good way to past the time, but on discovering that the 't' in my palms was significant and similar to what he described in his articles. I traveled to St. Andrew to find him.

I could not tell any other family member about this, just Vernon who accompanied me.

I was 28 at the time, married for twelve years, had three children, one of them, my dearest youngest boy Frederick died from typhoid fever just a few months earlier. I was still raw with grief.

Vernon and I had never ventured into the capital city before, and we were excited to experience what it was like to go to Kingston. It took my mind off my child's death for a while.

We took the train from Kendal to Kingston, and it was quite an experience. We had never been on a train before, and I was quite taken with the beauty of the interior hills.

We reached Kingston late afternoon after venturing out in the early morning. The train was so slow; it was a good thing we carried food for the journey.

When we found Oswald King's house, it was near night. The house was a white square edifice with brown shutters. There was a wrap around veranda at the top, which I assumed was to take advantage of the views.

Vernon was the one who knocked on the door. By this time we were feeling exhausted and not very confident in leaving our home just to pursue what was for us an unlikely adventure.

When Oswald King answered the door, Vernon pulled back; he wasn't expecting a tall, imposing white man to answer.

Oswald was stern looking, and heavily tanned with red patches on his face especially his nose. It was obvious that he spent hours in the sun. He was suspicious of us at first, but then I showed him my palms as we greeted he became very excited.

I have never been greeted so enthusiastically by a human being in my entire life.

He pressed us to stay for the night.

His housekeeper Mrs. Cotton was quite friendly too and told us that they didn't have many visitors. She cooked corned beef and served slices of it with cabbage and potatoes. It was Mr. King's favorite meal. He was half Irish on his mother's side.

Oswald King spoke all throughout dinner. He told us of his childhood, he told us of his marriage to a woman named Daisy who left him twice in each timeline and he told us everything about the resetters.

He had met many resetters in his life. He had been an army man and traveled the world.

It was an Irish cousin of his, Sean O'Sullivan who had seen his palms and told him that he was a resetter and what it meant.

It was also Sean O'Sullivan who gave him clues to where the pathways were in Jamaica.

He had gotten it off a sailor, who had gotten it from a pirate and this ancient map could be traced all the way to Sir Henry Morgan, who was rumored to be a resetter himself.

He showed us the pathway clues, and I readily recognized that one of the clues was linked to my land. I could barely contain my excitement.

Here they are:

'In a land that is cool, the stone is blue; palm-to-palm you'll know what to do.

'At the side of the road in plain sight covered in stone lays a resetter and his ride.'

'Nestled in a rock with grime and filth lays a gem in the midst of it, for a resetter do with it what he wilt.'

There is a stone on my land, which is blue; it has a palm print of sorts in there. I told Oswald King, and he was excited too, and then he sobered up.

He warned us that going back would not necessarily change the future for the better. He told us that resetters could go back anywhere in their lives even their birth.

He told us that resetters have been dabbling in time for centuries. Some were burnt at the stakes as witches and have been persecuted through the ages. *They tend to keep a low profile, many of them choosing not to travel back in time because it was more trouble than it was worth.*

He also said that resetters have made changes in political events but weren't very successful so far. He says that he has met resetters who tried to avert major disasters but ended up creating another. He told us that resetters should be mostly observers. Vernon and I retired late into the night unable to sleep.

Thinking about all we had learned and if it was true. We talked about going back and changing things for Frederick. We considered how blessed we were that the other children who had also gotten the fever had not died.

Suppose I went back and then all three of them died. Resetting was a gamble we were not willing to take.

When I got up in the morning, I was sure that resetting was not for me. But I am sure that there are other people braver than me who would do it. It is a powerful thing—having the ability to go back in time with prior knowledge. If you are a resetter and you want to go back here are all the facts that I learned from Oswald King.

Some facts about resetters:

Resetters are characterized by having a T in their palms. This is a very rare occurrence. Most resetters are not aware that they have this gift.

Resetters have to connect with a pathway. Pathways are usually made of stone. One known pathway is right in my backyard, the blue rock.

Resetters can take back some things with them including rings, watches, photographs, and notebooks. But only if it was produced or available in the time in which they went back to and only if these items are clutched in their palms.

Resetters usually forget their other life the longer they stay in the new one. For some people it happens quickly they only have a few days to reset, for others, there are exceptions to this rule.

Some resetters remember the other timeline clearly for the rest of their lives. Oswald King says he has met a few of them; they give him stories for his articles. They make predictions and are called prophets.

They sometimes prevent disasters.

Oswald King has met resetters who are coming from as far ahead as 1980. He heard that he would die Septemeber 1, 1957 from what is now known as the infamous train crash in Kendal.

He told us he would never ride that train again, he wouldn't leave his house in 1957, but apparently, he did. He was one of the casualties of that accident.

If you are a resetter and reading this, please note that you have a great responsibility on your hands, use it for good not evil.

*****

Travis glanced at the clock. It was nearing two o'clock in the morning. He couldn't believe that he had been so engrossed in the diary.

A newspaper article fell out of the book as he put it back on the side table. He saw that the folded pages was an article by Oswald King entitled, Resetters are Real. He rubbed his hand over his eyes and turned off the light. His mind was even more stimulated than when he started reading.

The main question in his head was, *What if it were true? What if it wasn't just fiction? What if resetters were real and that the lady who wrote the diary, Oswald King and Sky weren't just living under some grand delusion?*

What if he could go back and this was not just some fantasy?

It was the last thought on his mind as he drifted off. He didn't even hear the alarm as it went off for him to go swimming.

Chapter Eleven

"**A**re you okay?" Sky asked him a couple of nights later. She had her eyes closed. A lone textbook opened on her chest.

"How was your exam today?" He glanced at her and then back at his computer screen.

"Terrible." Sky opened her eyes to a slit and glanced at him. "Your exam that is, the other one was easy."

Travis smiled. "It was multiple choice. How can multiple choice be terrible?"

"Hardy-har." Sky closed her eyes again. "One exam to go and then I am seriously going to vegetate after I go shopping with Monica for work clothes."

"Getting along with your stepmom?"

"She suggested it," Sky grunted. "They are so excited that I am going to be working in Kingston. My dad has no problems with me staying with you. Apparently, he thinks you are harmless."

"I do give off a harmless vibe. Travis grinned. "It's the wheelchair."

"You didn't answer my question though," Sky turned on her side and looked at him, "As absorbed as I have been with the books these last few days I can tell when you are not okay."

"I am okay." Travis turned away from the folder filled with old photocopied newspaper articles from Oswald Kings. "When you are done with all your exams, we talk."

"We talk now," Sky said eagerly. "I could probably do Financial Management in my sleep. You are so much more interesting, Dr. Jefferson." She batted her eyelashes at him and then laughed.

Travis grinned with her. He liked watching her laugh. She was dressed in an oversized heather gray dress with a hoodie. Her hair was in a topknot and her face bare of makeup. She looked adorable and carefree, and he loved her.

The realization was like a sucker punch to his gut. He knew he liked her... but love? He had gotten her that job so that he could have her close for the summer. He offered her a place to stay in his apartment because he wanted to see her every day. He never wanted to let her go, to let her out of his sight.

How did this intense feeling come about?

He inhaled ruggedly and tried to clear his head.

"I read Mrs. Gwendolyn Fisher Campbell's resetter book. Fantastic stuff."

"You did!" Sky sat up, and her dress rode up on her legs.

"And I read the article from Oswald King, and then I went to the library and photocopied all of the stories he wrote for the Daily Paper."

"And," Sky was practically bouncing on the seat in excitement.

"And it is disturbing." Travis wheeled closer to her until

they were knee to knee.

"Good," Sky said smugly.

He reached out and tucked a tendril of hair behind her ears. "It would be ironic that I am tempted to go back to the past when the present finally makes sense for me now."

Sky leaned into him until they were almost touching nose to nose. "Really now? What is it about the present that is so fascinating?"

"You," Travis said huskily.

He caressed the nape of her neck and brought her even closer to him. "You are still my student. Well, until I hand in your final grades."

He kissed her lightly on the lips and then released her.

Sky was having none of that she moved off the settee and sat in his lap putting her legs over the chair.

"You have an erection." She murmured in his ear. "I can feel it."

"They don't last long," he whispered back hoarsely. "I can't believe I am telling you this."

"Who else would you tell?" Sky pulled back and smiled at him.

"We wouldn't have a normal sex life." He looked at her seriously, "Sky, we can't..."

Sky placed a finger on his lips. "Normal is overrated."

Travis looked at her solemnly. "No, it is not. Normal is making love to you properly; normal is not feeling guilty while I burden you with my limitations. You are young and gorgeous, and you have your whole life ahead of you. Normal at your age should be important."

Sky rested her head on his chest. "My cousin Addi said that in 2017, twenty-one years from now, I killed myself."

"What?" Travis asked incredulously. "Why?"

"Because I was unhappy." Sky murmured. "I was apparently

a high powered business woman with a fat bank account and all the lovely things the world could offer. Apparently, I found out that the guy I spent a good chunk of my life pining over was paid by my mother to kill my father."

"Oh, that story," Travis gripped her tighter.

Sky clutched him tighter and sighed. "We stopped the plot to kill him in its tracks, and so he is still alive."

She looked up at Travis earnestly. "The point is, in my previous life I was unhappy. I don't want to be unhappy this time around. The truth is, you make me happy. I don't care that you are in a wheelchair or that your erection may not last more than a couple of seconds."

Travis grimaced. "It hurts when you say it out loud like that."

"All I know," Sky looked at him seriously, "is that I love you. I don't think this is a crush either or some fleeting feeling based on teenage hormones or even an overactive sex drive."

Travis clutched her closer to him after that speech, his heart feeling as if it was going to burst in his chest with gratitude and hope.

He kissed her in her hair. "I love you too, Sky."

****

One week after exams and one day before her new job and Sky was spending all her time with Travis in his apartment, mostly in bed, sometimes without. It was only natural that when the doorbell rang early on Sunday that she pulled on one of Travis' shirts and opened the door without thinking.

"You!" Amelia Perkins screeched.

Sky blinked at her blearily. "Keep it down Travis is sleeping."

"For goodness sake!" Amelia looked livid. "You live with him?"

"Not really." Sky leaned on the doorjamb. "It feels like it sometimes. I stay over here more than my own apartment."

She watched as Amelia's ears reddened about three shades darker.

"He is going to lose his job over you." Amelia hissed. "Because I am going to report this. This is way beyond the pale. There are rumors, and then there is this...evidence. I have seen with my own eyes that Travis is having a relationship with his student. This is wrong!"

"Okay, keep it down," Sky muttered groggily. She had been up late into the night watching old taped movies with Travis.

"Did you stop by for something in particular?"

"I came to personally invite him to my niece's christening." Amelia sputtered, "but he can forget that now. I am through with Travis Jefferson. He obviously has no morals. He is sleeping with a student."

Sky rolled her eyes. "You said that already."

"Deny it," Amelia said beseechingly, "do something to at least save his reputation. Because I am not joking when I say I am going to the university president with this. You might be a little remorseful too. You will cause a man to lose his job."

Sky raised an eyebrow. "But I am not the one running to tell."

"What do you get out of this?" Amelia asked. "We all know that in a few weeks you'll be leaving him for someone else, someone whole. Young people have the attention span of a gnat, and you look as flaky as the best of them."

"What I don't understand," Sky retorted, "is why you keep trying to insert yourself in his life every chance you get if you hold Travis in such low esteem and think he is so unlovable. I might look flaky but I love him, and I am not going to leave him for anyone else, as far as I am concerned he is whole."

She closed the door before she said something else rude to the woman who was going to be teaching her Macro Economics that summer. She turned and bumped into Travis. He was right behind her shirtless; his hair tousled; his eyes still sleepy.

"You look good in my shirt." He took her hand and pulled her down on his lap.

"I have her for Econ in my second summer session," Sky whispered mortified as Travis cupped her naked breast under the shirt.

"Forget her," Travis whispered. "This is going to be a good morning for you."

Sky's squeals could be heard through the closed apartment door.

Amelia stopped on the landing and clenched her teeth in anger.

Chapter Twelve

Travis' apartment in new Kingston was on the top floor of an eight-story building that was wheelchair friendly.

"My father built it," Travis explained when he was wheeling down the spacious hallways toward his apartment. "He amended the designs to accommodate persons with disabilities because his son was suddenly a cripple. Funny how our perspective changes when we are faced with situations like these, huh."

Sky nodded. She was pulling along her suitcase beside him, suddenly feeling apprehensive and a little overwhelmed.

Travis was in a strange mood ever since they arrived in New Kingston. He had gotten more solemn. He was stony-faced when they approached apartment 315. There were six apartments on the top floor, all of them occupied by family members who worked at the firm.

He pushed a key in the door and wheeled inside before her. "Welcome."

He gave her a genuine smile and Sky exhaled in relief. For a minute there she was wondering if she was in trouble or he was rethinking having her around.

"Thank you." She walked past him and into an open plan apartment that was large, airy and very luxurious, with a white and gray décor. There were red vases with plants, which gave the room some color.

A bank of glass doors opened up to a large patio where there was a table and chairs.

"Wow." Sky whispered looking around. She headed to the patio and saw the view of the St Andrew hills in the distance. *It was gorgeous.*

"Mr. Travis!" a female voice said behind her. Sky spun around and saw a Grace Jones look-alike in a white crochet dress and broad hat approaching Travis with a smile.

"June," Travis said pleasantly. "I didn't expect to see you here today."

"I am just coming from church," June said glancing at Sky. "You must be Miss Skyler. I am June."

She came closer to Sky and held out her hand for a handshake and Sky took it.

"If you folks are hungry I have baked chicken in the fridge, glazed sweet potatoes and rice and peas."

"Thank you June, we'll help ourselves," Travis said waving her off. "It's your time off. Where's Milly?"

"Milly disappeared two days ago," June said heavily, "I was hoping she would be back by today."

Travis sighed. "Really, why didn't you tell me?"

June looked contrite. "Her mother came to visit, and they fought."

"What about?" Travis muttered. "Why would Marla fight with Milly when she is in a fragile state of mind?"

"I think it was supposed to be a friendly visit," June said

heavily, "and the next thing I know they were fighting about her irresponsibility, her drug use, her friends...Milly broke a couple of your figurines throwing them at Marla. I had to hide out for a time, while she vented her anger on the place."

"Good grief." Travis looked pained.

"This family has more trouble than a whore going to church on Sunday," June muttered, "and to think that y'all are rich."

Sky stifled a giggle.

June turned around and looked at her. "It's true Miss Skyler; the Jefferson's are not blessed with peace and tranquility. Money can't buy this family happiness."

"I have to find Milly." Travis wheeled toward the phone on the center table and ignored both Sky and June.

June looked at Sky. "Well let me show you to your room. No need to just stand around while Mr. Travis searches for his sister."

Sky looked at Travis with concern, but he was already talking to somebody from a security company.

"Mr. Travis loves his sister," June said heading down the hallway and opening a door to a spacious bedroom in blue and white. "Milly is just five years older than he is you know. They practically grew up together."

Sky nodded. "So she's a drug addict?"

"Yes ma'am, got into the habit as a teenager. She was a functioning addict for years until Mr. Travis got into that accident. She got worse, doesn't handle grief well. It's a wonder she is still alive. She has been in one scrape after another and on the brink of death time and again."

"So what does Mr. Jefferson do about it?" Sky asked, "Her father?"

"He pays for her rehab and then ignores her," June opened the patio doors to the room. "He doesn't handle crisis well. He keeps his head in the sand. He likes when the women deal with the home life.

"He ain't gonna get no father of the year award." June snorted. "They had an article in the papers the other day about how he was an exemplary father. I laughed until I cried.

"The oldest daughter, Beth, doesn't speak to him, the second one, Carly, is more interested in her sons getting ahead in the company than a relationship with him, so she sucks up to him. You can see she hates it.

"Mr. Travis is crippled and rejected the business all together. They haven't spoken in years. Milly is a druggie and the illegitimate son, Duke, is obviously a user. He might be the worst one. You can just take one look at him and know that he is up to no good. He has revenge in his heart."

Sky sat on one of the blue armchairs her eyes wide. "Wow, Travis didn't tell me the situation was so er...dire."

June shrugged. "People don't like speaking ill of their folks, but you should hear it, aren't you going to be working with Mr. Miguel for the summer?"

"Yes." Sky swallowed. "I am."

"Then you should know what kind of man he is," June warned. "He may be good with the dollars, but with his own family he has no sense."

****

By Monday morning Sky was pretty nervous. She twisted and turned in the mirror to get a better look at her dark blue suit.

Her eyes strayed to her hair; maybe she should have put it in a bun. Wearing it out seemed a bit too casual.

"This is not your first job, is it?" Travis asked sleepily from the bed as she looked into the mirror one more time to make sure that she looked presentable.

"I have only ever worked for the family," Sky said pulling the brush through her curls one last time. "How do I look?"

"Gorgeous," Travis said, "so good in fact that I am rethinking you working for my dad."

"Is he a womanizer?" Sky asked widening her eyes.

"No," Travis murmured. "It's the young execs you need to look out for, the ones who will be swooping in and out of the office. They will offer to take you out on dates. They'll act like little kids in a candy store when they see you."

Sky laughed. "Don't worry; I only have eyes for you."

She kissed him on the forehead. "Love you, babe."

"Love you too." Travis held her hand when she was about to leave. "I'll have June move your things in here; it's ridiculous to pretend that you are sleeping in the guest room."

"Fine." Sky looked at him contemplatively. "Last night you didn't sleep much."

"My sister is on the streets." Travis sighed. "I am worried. When the security company finds her, I am going to put her under house arrest."

"I am looking forward to meeting her," Sky said standing up. "Got to go."

"I might come by today, around lunchtime." Travis ran his fingers through his hair. "Say hello to my dad, maybe we can go for lunch."

"Sure thing." Sky nodded. "See you soon."

****

Miguel Jefferson's office was not a typical office; Sky thought it looked like a mini apartment. It had a desk, a mini-golf course a leather couch, a conference table and was carpeted in a plush brown carpet that looked like it would be hell to clean.

The man himself was tall, dark brown complexioned and fit looking. He looked familiar like she had seen him somewhere before.

She mentioned this out loud after the introduction to him when she was alone with Betsy, his personal secretary, and she laughed.

"I think it's because he looks little like Harry Belafonte, don't you think?"

Sky shook her head. "No."

Betsy shrugged. "When you figure it out tell me."

And thus her orientation into the world of Jefferson Pharmaceutical began. Betsy was a pleasant lady who looked to be in her mid-fifties or something. She was on a first name basis with her boss and ran a tight ship that much was obvious. She was also very thankful for the summer help.

Sky was given her own desk in Betsy's office, which was Mr. Jefferson's outer office and was assigned a months worth of filing, but first, she had to arrange the files according to dates.

She was given a crash course on how to answer the telephone and what Mr. Jefferson liked for breakfast, lunch, and dinner. She was introduced to quite a few persons who had appointments with Miguel Jefferson. Men and women who looked like high-powered movers and shakers.

They all treated Betsy as the gatekeeper of the inner sanctum, all except for one particular imposing gentleman who came to the outer office. He was as tall as Miguel Jefferson. They had similar looking square jaws.

Betsy was on the phone when he stopped by so he ignored

her and looked at Sky.

"Is the old man in there with anyone?"

"Not that I know of." Sky shrugged and went back to her filing.

She could see from the corner of her eye that he narrowed his eyes. "What's your name?"

"Skyler Porter," Sky said unsmilingly. She was getting a bad vibe from this guy. He was handsome and clean-shaven. He had light brown eyes, and he was cold.

He had an arrogant look and a twist of distaste to his mouth like she was the manor maid who had just sassed her overlord.

He folded his arm over his chest and raised an eyebrow. "And this is your first day?"

"Yes." Sky suppressed her annoyance, but some of it shone through.

He frowned and was about to say something when Betsy came off the phone.

"Sorry, Duke. Miguel has a ten o'clock with the South American people. That's what I was setting up."

"Drat it." Duke sighed. "What time can I come back, I need to talk to him about Trinidad."

"About eleven or lunchtime," Betsy said picking up the phone again when it rang.

He glanced at her and Sky could feel his stony regard.

When he walked over to the desk and glowered down at her, she felt nervous. This was Travis' illegitimate brother, the housekeeper's son. The one who was making a power play to run the company?

"Who is your contact?" Duke asked her unsmilingly.

"Excuse me." Sky frowned looking up at him with as bad a glower as his.

"The coveted assistant job to Betsy is usually filled by

close friends of Miguel Jefferson's circle of exalted friends. Who pulled strings for you to be here?"

"That is none of your business," Sky said coldly.

"Do you know who I am?" Duke hissed.

"No." Sky sneered. "Should I?"

"You insubordinate..." Duke stepped back from the desk. "You just lost your job."

Sky smiled at him coldly. "It won't be the end of the world, will it? Life will go on. You, on the other hand, will still be cold, arrogant and ignorant."

Duke pointed at her. "By the end of the day, you are out of here!"

Betsy put down the phone and looked at Sky and then the retreating back of Duke, "What's wrong?"

Sky inhaled twice before she could calm down her racing heart. She hated confrontation, and in her opinion, this one was uncalled for.

"He asked me who pull strings to get me this job and I told him it was none of his business and he lost it. Said I would be out of here by the end of the day."

Betsy frowned. "Usually he doesn't act so volatile. It really was none of his business. Firing you is my purview, not his, don't worry. Though next time, be polite, he is the vice president of operations. He has Miguel's ear. How is the filing going?"

"Good," Sky said looking down at the pile on her desk.

"Then we are good." Betsy went back to typing up some document or the other and Sky exhaled tremulously.

If she were fired today surely that would be some record.

****

Travis wheeled down the hallway toward his father's

office. It was the first time he was going to see him since Christmas holidays. At that time his father had tried to avoid him like he had some communicable disease.

His father was an inadequate parent at the best of times. His disabled son made him uncomfortable.

Travis sighed. He wasn't looking forward to this meeting. They had agreed to have lunch. One hour out of Miguel Jefferson's busy day. He had no idea what they were going to talk about for that long.

He was surprised to see that when he arrived at the outer office where Betsy held the fort that Sky was not there and Betsy looked frazzled.

Betsy was never frazzled.

"Hi Travis, I double booked Miguel for lunch. Duke wanted to see him."

Travis raised an eyebrow. "Where is Sky?"

"I sent her to run an errand in Finance." Betsy groaned and looked over his head a painful expression on her face.

"Duke, I was just telling Travis that I double booked you both for Miguel."

Travis spun around and regarded Duke who was staring at him transfixed.

"What are you doing here?" Duke finally asked.

"Just checking on my dad, having lunch, catching up," Travis said stressing the 'my dad' and liking the way that Duke winced.

"I have business to discuss," Duke growled impatiently. "I take precedence over your little girly chat."

Travis laughed and spun around to Betsy. "Tell my father that I am here and Duke is here. Let's see who he decides to see."

Betsy picked up the phone looking between the two men as they waited. Travis glanced at Duke. He was nervous!

This little game of choice was important to him. Travis was confident though that his dad would see him. His mother had already made the call and practically threatened him to see Travis.

His mother had more clout than the pharmaceutical governing board where his father was concerned.

Betsy hung up the phone and looked at Travis. "He said you should come in. Duke, he is asking that you talk first thing tomorrow."

Travis wheeled toward his father's office. Not before looking back at the murderous look of darkness that had descended over Duke's face.

Travis smirked. "By the way how is Melanie?"

Duke schooled his features into the semblance of a smile. "She is quite fine."

Travis decided to goad him. "Milly said that since you two got married, Melanie has been stepping out on you with the whole board of Jefferson Pharmaceutical."

Duke clenched his teeth in barely concealed rage. "Milly is a drug addict whose brain probably has more holes than cheese. I wouldn't put stock in anything she says."

"But it does make you wonder though," Travis said contemplatively as he pushed the door and went into his father's office. "Melanie has always been a good time girl."

****

"I wish you would get along with Duke," Miguel said when he wheeled into the office.

"Why?" Travis asked stopping his chair right in front of the desk

"Because he is a good man." Miguel cleared his throat and then rested back in his chair and looked at Travis. "He is going to succeed me as president of this company."

"Because I am crippled," Travis said curling his hands around the chair.

"No, because he is my son and he works here. He cares about the business. You don't." Miguel growled.

"So you finally admit he's your son."

"And I noticed you don't look shocked." Miguel sighed. "I guess you knew for a while now."

"No." Travis gritted out, "I found out when a reporter told me a few weeks ago."

"It wasn't a secret." Miguel shrugged. "It was bound to come out one day. Now you know."

Travis squinted his eyes and looked at him. "It was a secret. You are just acting nonchalant about it because you want somebody of your blood to succeed you and in your screwed up mind, Duke is the only legitimate candidate, because some perceived criteria disqualify all your other children. You have no clue how to be a father do you?" Miguel laughed dryly. "It doesn't exactly come written in a manual. If you weren't crippled and in hiding, I wouldn't have to resort to having Duke succeed me."

"There!" Travis held up his hand in exasperation. "Dad, the reason I am not working in this company is you. You believe that since I can't feel my legs, my brain can't be working. You wrote me off ten years ago. I had no encouragement to stick around here. I proved myself time and again that I could do things. I got my doctorate. I teach at a university!"

"I don't want to argue with you," Miguel said soothingly, "I really don't. Why is it that every time I meet with a member of this family, there is an argument?"

"Because you suck at being empathetic," Travis said frankly. "You have lost touch with your family members. Your own offspring."

"You all are a mess." Miguel snorted, "I don't have time for messes."

"Milly is missing," Travis said heavily.

"Milly is always missing." Miguel snorted. "When she is found again, I will pay for her rehab as usual. She is a money pit. The most exasperating, ungrateful, unthankful..."

Travis looked at him solemnly. "How did you get like this?"

"How?" Miguel growled. His phone rang, and he ignored it.

"You were never this bad, one time when I was younger you were nice. You used to take Duke and me to cricket games, you taught us how to drive, you were around, and we could talk to you. Though at the time I had no idea that Duke was your son. I was feeling lucky that my dad could be so available to my fatherless friend. I didn't mind sharing you with him at all. You should have told me."

Miguel sighed. "I couldn't. Children don't keep secrets well. They tend to blab."

He drummed his fingers on the desk. "I might as well tell you..."

The phone rang again, and he held up his hand and barked into it. "What?"

When he hung up, he looked at Travis sheepishly. "The lunch is here. Let's go over to the table."

****

Travis had no appetite for the well-prepared spread. He nibbled on the grapes from the fruit platter while his father ate the salmon and salad.

"You were going to tell me something," Travis said after a

few minutes of silence.

Miguel pushed away his plate and sighed. "1976, you were eleven, Duke was ten. The cold formula was going well; I had just got it trademarked. The business was taking off and doing great but that February, I'll never forget it. Munro Smith, my friend, my best friend, and chief accountant left the company."

"I don't remember him." Travis frowned.

"That's because he didn't leave the company empty-handed. For a full year, he siphoned off the money from the company, piece by piece. By the time he left, there was nothing left, and I had a load of debt miles high."

Miguel snorted. "If I had just paid attention to AJ Sullivan, he had been in my skin for months to get the books audited. I didn't listen because I thought that Munro was doing a wonderful job."

Travis nodded. "A.J. is the best in his field. Still is."

"The best." Miguel agreed. "Anyway, after Munro ran off with the money, it's as if all the bad things that could happen to me happened. It was a watershed year, I tell you. First, Arlene started agitating for me to tell the world about Duke but what she really wanted was for me to tell your mother.

"Your grandfather had offered to give me a loan to cover the shortfall because he realized I was in deep. I was desperate at that point, to be honest, so I accepted. I had creditors knocking at my door; we were going to lose the house.

"And then in the midst of the turmoil I had to be working at the office, I had three households to take care of.

"Marla was pressuring me to spend more time with the girls; Arlene was threatening to tell Pasha about Duke. You were looking at me with those big sad eyes, *Daddy, why can't we play ball on Sundays?*

"I was always working. I had to. I had no choice.

"If Arlene blabbed about Duke, your mother would leave. Your grandfather wouldn't give me the loan. We would probably be living penniless in a tenement yard in Kingston. So, I paid Arlene to shut up. Like a greedy pig, she took the money and stopped insisting that I spend time with Duke like I spend time with you, and she kept the secret about Duke from Pasha.

"I bought Marla her precious pottery business so she would stop badgering me too. By '78 we were back in the black, but by that time I realized that the women in my life were mercenary."

"What about my mom?" Travis asked hoarsely.

Miguel wiped his mouth and then answered. "Your grandfather's loan was for a 30% stake in the business. It passed to her when he died in '82, which makes your mother an equal shareholder to me.

Don't for one minute believe that she isn't as mercenary as the other two. In the last couple of months that I told her I wanted Duke to succeed me, I have seen another side of Pasha I didn't know existed."

"I didn't know about any of this," Travis folded his arms contemplatively.

Miguel sighed. "This whole thing has turned into a numbers game. With four children with 5% shares and other investors at 20%. Your mother and I are on equal footing as far as decision making for the next president is concerned.

"If I vote for Duke to succeed and the investors vote likewise that's 50% against 50%. A tie."

"Are you sure that Carly and Elizabeth won't back you on this?" Travis asked,

Miguel laughed harshly. "They have both stopped speaking to me. I think Carly might, her children work here after all, but Milly will vote for anybody you vote for."

"I can't vote for Duke," Travis said abruptly. "He was evil to me when we were younger. He has always hated me, and I didn't even know it. He has always wanted to be your only son. He has tried everything to get me to fail even drugs."

"You could have fought back." Miguel hissed. "Good God man, grow a pair."

"It is easy to fight when you know who your enemy is. I had no idea he had some sort of brotherly vendetta against me. He is ultimately the reason I am in this chair!"

"No, he is not. Your stupidity is the reason why you are in that chair!" Miguel stood up and threw down his napkin.

He looked through the window, "Duke is a sly competitor, a cutthroat businessman. He is the best man for the job. Not a whiner like..."

"Me," Travis inhaled roughly, "too bad for you. This whiner has more say in your business than you do."

Miguel looked at him with furrowed brow. "You have a point. Report for work tomorrow, and I'll see if you can handle this job. Otherwise, I am going to have to go to war with my own wife, and it won't be pretty."

Chapter Thirteen

And nd here is a new release from Donna Lewis, I Love You
Always Forever, the announcer said over the radio. *It sounds
like this one is going to be a hit this summer.*

Sky had the radio blasting on Power 106, while she washed
her hair. It was a week since she started the new job and
almost a week since Travis had also taken up residence in the
office across from his father's.

She thought that she would see more of him, but she was
mistaken. This Sunday morning she was alone at home as he
had left already to go to some important meeting with some
bigwigs.

She wrung her hair dry and walked out of the shower into
the bedroom and screamed. A woman was sitting in one of
the armchairs in the bedrooms as still as a statue staring into
space.

She didn't react immediately to Sky's screams, which had
a ridiculously calming effect on Sky.

"Who are you?" Sky finally croaked.

The lady looked at her lazily. "They call me Milly, which is short for Millicent." Her voice was raspy and sounded like sandpaper on wood.

"Oh," Sky widened her eyes. This woman looked much older than thirty-six. She was skinny, almost emaciated. She had very light skin and dime sized red marks all over her face. Her lips were black, and she had a dead look in her eyes. Like her eyelids were too lazy to be raised much further than she had them.

"I had to take a break," Milly said conversationally, "escape from here for a while." She sighed and looked at Sky. "Who are you?"

"Sky." Sky pulled the robe closer to her, "I am staying here for the summer."

Milly shrugged one bony shoulder. "My brother has a lover? Good for him."

She got up. "I have to go get some shut-eye. Tell my brother I am home. He can call off the dogs."

She left the room, closing the door behind her.

Sky sat down on the bed heavily, the towel on her hair slipped off, and she took it up and absently squeezed her hair.

Milly was not how she imagined she would be. Her head barely looked like her neck could support it. And she moved slowly, way too slowly for a woman her age.

She picked up the phone to call Travis at the office and listened for it to ring. She almost hung up when it rang more than five times, but he finally answered.

"Hey," Sky said briskly, "bad time?"

"Not really." Travis sighed down the phone. "My father is driving me crazy but apart from that...oh and my mom is inviting us to dinner."

Sky gasped. "Me? She knows about me?"

"Yes. She knows." Travis chuckled. "Pick you up at three. Don't worry she won't bite."

"Don't go yet," Sky said hurriedly. "Your sister is back."

"I heard a few moments ago," Travis said grimly. "The security firm I hired to look for her, found her in a ghetto with one of Jamaica's most wanted. They got her out of there before tipping the police. He was so wanted that there was a million dollars bounty on his head."

"Wow," Sky gasped. "No wonder Milly looks like hell."

"I can imagine." Travis sighed. "My dad is insisting that she goes to rehab. The apartment is guarded till then."

Sky hung up the phone. She was a little apprehensive to go outside into the hall. She was a little afraid of Milly but she had five hours to burn until dinner. She wanted to read the Sunday Paper and then watch a movie.

She eventually developed some courage and crept out of the room and her heart sank as she saw that Milly was in the living room sitting and looking out at the mountain view.

"Don't mind me," Milly said without turning around. "I might look like death warmed up but I am not contagious, and I do smell good, had a shower just now. I just can't sleep. Too many bad images in my head."

Sky went further into the room and picked up the paper.

"You want to know why I am this way?" Milly asked Sky conversationally after she perused the papers and her nose in the business section. Trying to remember if any of the news she was reading was familiar from her time travel book.

"Huh?" Sky looked up.

"Why I am this way," Milly repeated, "drugged up, battered look like this. Don't have two senses to rub together."

"I well er..." Sky lowered the paper, "why?"

"Because of a guy," Milly said turning fully to face Sky.

"Ramone Jarrett."

"Okay," Sky nodded.

"I was at my father's house hanging with my brother and his friends. One of them, the guy with the deep voice, the one with the keloid skin and the broad mouth was my nemesis.

"He wasn't particularly attractive like in a classical way. He was the kind of guy that you looked at, and you knew he was trouble. Maybe that was his appeal. He was from the wrong side of the tracks; you could smell it on him.

"He was my age and didn't have a job, and he smelled like marijuana. I lusted after him. Uptown girl with all the opportunities at her disposal and I chose Ramone Jarrett."

Sky looked at her interestedly. Milly was speaking like someone who had all her wits about her.

Milly seemed to read her mind and chuckled. "I can't remember much of last week, but I remember him. I'll remember him forever. I have a thing for bad boys, and he was the baddest of them all.

"He killed a man in front of me."

Sky gasped.

"Yeah," Milly said unmoved. "And he introduced me to the hard stuff cocaine and all of that. I slept with his friends while he watched. I even slept with Duke."

Milly made a face. "Heard he was my brother a couple of weeks ago. Now I feel gross. I never thought I had it in me anymore to feel gross."

Sky put down the paper completely. Milly had her undivided attention.

"I worked at a bank then, went to all the parties, told them who in my crowd to rob. I even helped them when they robbed my bank." Milly laughed lightly, "and then Ramone found some other patsy to do his dirty work and I was no longer attractive to him. I was a washed up drugged up has been.

"He kicked me out of his apartment, told me that he paid Duke too much for me."

Sky frowned. "What?"

"Yep, I was sold to Ramone. I didn't even know I was for sale by Duke of all people."

Milly nodded and then went back into silence. Like her story had taken her too much effort.

Sky picked up the paper again.

"He was killed," Milly said nearly half an hour later.

Sky lowered the paper again.

"Gang violence." Milly continued. "I was in rehab. I relapsed."

Silence again. This time Milly started rocking.

"You ever tell anyone about this Milly?" Sky asked gently.

Milly didn't answer. She looked at Sky. "I am going to kill Duke. He is the reason I am like this. One day I am going to kill him. You can't just sell people."

Sky didn't respond. She didn't know how to react that passionate outburst.

She almost jumped higher than the chair when there was a knock on the door, and then it was opened. June came in, her smile bright. She was dressed in her church clothes.

"Hello there, Miss Sky. Miss Milly."

Milly ignored her.

"Hello," Sky said in relief.

June looked at Sky. "Mr. Travis asked me to come over, said you probably would feel odd being her alone with Milly."

June must have read the relief on Sky's face because she chuckled and came over to sit by Sky. "What's in the news?"

"More of the same." Sky handed her the stack of papers and went to the kitchen for a snack.

****

"Who is Ramone Jarrett?" Sky asked Travis when they were heading to his parent's house in the hills.

"Ramone Jarrett, I haven't heard that name in a long time." Travis looked at Sky and then back on the road.

"He was one of Duke's cronies when my mom got Arlene fired they lived in the inner-city for a while with Arlene's cousin. I think her name was Peaches. Ramone, Randy, and Reese, the three R's were Peaches children.

"They didn't have good role models growing up, but they used to seem so cool to me. I can't understand why now. Maybe because they talked tough and seemed like they had the kind of freedom that a teenaged boy like myself didn't have and when they conversed they spoke about a world so alien to mine, it was fascinating to listen to, even though it was mostly crap.

"They barely made it out of their teenage years. I know Ramone died in a gang-related turf war years ago.

Rocky is probably somewhere out there doing God knows what, and Reese is in prison—on death row.

"Why did you ask about Ramone?"

"Because your sister said he was the one who led her into taking drugs. Apparently, Duke sold her to Ramone."

Sky went on to tell Travis the conversation she had with Milly. When she was done, Travis looked shell-shocked. He slowed to a crawl on his way up the hill.

"She has never said that to me," he whispered. "Those three guys and Duke were not my friends. They were always with Duke, and he'd carry them to hang with us. They were the ones who started me drinking and smoking too."

Sky snorted, "Duke is just bad news."

"I think he could have been a better person if his father had acknowledged him. If he wasn't made to feel like an outsider for most of his life. He must have resented us."

Travis sighed. "We were the children who had the Jefferson name who probably had everything he never had."

Sky glanced at him. "It's nice of you to empathize with his story but let me tell you, he is rotten to the core and if what your sister said was true he is worse than I thought."

****

Pasha Jefferson was a pleasant surprise for Sky and instantly put her at ease. They were greeted in the large foyer of the marble tiled mansion that the Jefferson's called their home. Pasha was short. She wore a red sari, and she had her hair in one jet-black plait all the way down to her hips.

Miguel Jefferson was different too. He was much more relaxed than when she saw him at the office. He was dressed in polo shirt and jeans; he led them into the open ceiling living room and proceeded to talk about sports.

There was no mention of the office, just polite banter. Sky watched Travis as he interacted with his parents.

His mother was obviously besotted with him. His father was more aloof.

Pasha was the one who cooked the entire Sunday dinner. There was enough food for an army.

And so many new dishes that Sky had never tried like Aloo Gobi and Vegetable Masala and Curried Beef in Pumpkin.

It was a gastronomical delight. Sky couldn't resist moaning when she tasted samples of some of the dishes.

Pasha laughed and beamed at her. "I like her, Travis!"

The warm family moment was broken when they heard a knock on the door.

Miguel went to answer, and he came back with Duke, ho was dressed in jeans and a polo shirt that had the Jackson company logo.

He was accompanied by a woman who looked like she was ripped right out of the centerfold of a magazine. Perfect skin, perfect hair, and perfect smile. She was dressed in a blue crochet dress that was off the shoulder and over her knees.

"Hello everyone," she greeted them huskily.

She looked at Travis and then Sky, dismissing her with a glance she looked back to Travis. "How are you all, this lovely Sunday?"

"We are doing well," Pasha said the distaste heavy in her voice.

"I won't stay long," Duke registered the dismissal in Pasha's stance, and his eyes flicked to the table, "I see you are having a cozy family moment."

He looked at Sky with cold hostility. She hadn't seen him all week since he threatened to fire her.

He held up a briefcase. "I just came for Miguel to sign these documents I am off to Trinidad for the next couple of weeks. I will be back for your birthday though, Miguel."

Miguel nodded and then got up. "Let's go to the study. Excuse me, everyone."

Melanie sat in the chair he vacated and then looked at Travis. "Well, you still look gorgeous."

Travis quirked his lip. "Thank you."

"And you, Pasha. You have got to cut down on the carbs you consume. You are looking a little round!" Melanie looked at Pasha and exclaimed.

Pasha glared at her. "As usual you tread where few people fear to go. Thank you for your very impolite observation about my weight."

Melanie laughed like it was a joke. "Somebody has to tell

you. Might as well be me, I am practically family, am I not?"

She then looked at Sky. "So who is this young looking ingénue?"

Travis was the one to answer. "My girlfriend."

Sky looked at him swiftly and started to smile.

Melanie looked between the two of them and cackled.

"Oh heavens, I never imagined you could have one of those! I thought your thing was broken!" And then in fake sympathy said, "You had to rob the cradle to get a little comfort dear Travis. I empathize."

Sky concluded right then and there that Melanie wasn't that pretty.

When Melanie and Duke left the evening became much more pleasant.

Chapter Fourteen

"**Y**ou dated her?" Sky asked Travis, accusation rife in her voice on Monday morning when they were getting ready for work.

"I was young and stupid." Travis pulled Sky down into his lap. "And that was years ago. Are you going to let this go? We already had this conversation yesterday, and last night."

"She still thinks you are gorgeous," Sky complained smoothing back Travis' hair, "and that's worrying."

"What's worrying is Duke." Travis sighed. "He is working on the Trinidad expansion like a man who is almost certain that he is going to get the big reward—president of the company."

Sky made a face. "Is he going to get it?"

"He can't," Travis frowned, "I have the weight of the shareholders behind me. My dad can't make that decision alone, but I think he told Duke that he could."

"Oh," Sky widened her eyes and then started to chuckle.

"Good for you bad for Duke."

"Which makes him dangerous," Travis said solemnly, "I wouldn't put it past him to do something about this situation. My dad is going to make an announcement on his birthday about his successor. Duke is going to be disappointed."

"He doesn't look like a person to be feared. He just looks like an arrogant stuck up jerk." Sky got up from Travis' lap. "I am looking forward to seeing his face when the succession is announced."

"Somehow I am not." Travis sighed. "He shouldn't be underestimated. He is after all my father's son.

That thought was at the back of Travis' mind all week. It was especially prominent when Duke came back from Trinidad.

Duke poked his head around Travis' office on Friday. "Remember Winston, the guy that you met in the accident with?"

Travis was in the middle of making sense of a contract with a supplier. He looked up.

"Yes."

"He is dead," Duke said smugly. "I told his dear grieving mother that you are working here at Jefferson's for the summer as alive and well as you please. While her dear Winston is dead."

Travis closed his eyes in remorse. *Poor Winston*. He had gotten the bad end of that accident.

"If you wish you were the one that is dead instead," Duke said from the door, "that can be arranged."

Travis opened his eyes and looked at him.

"It wouldn't be hard," Duke shrugged, "your legs are dead already I could take care of the next half easily."

"Are you threatening me?" Travis squinted his eyes and looked at Duke.

"No, just offering you some consolation in your time of grief." Duke smiled stiffly. "What exactly are you doing here?"

"What?" Travis frowned.

"What are you doing here in this office in this building, working with my...working with Miguel?" Duke corrected himself quickly.

"Ah," Travis caught his gaffe and decided to taunt him in retaliation for breaking the news about Winston so callously and coldly.

"He hasn't given you the permission to call him father in public, has he?"

A pained expression crossed Duke's face, but just as quickly as it appeared it left.

"This company is owned by shareholders."

He watched as Duke straightened up from the doorframe. "All of my father's children have shares, 5% each, he has four legitimate, acknowledged children, so that's 20% of the shares."

Duke swallowed.

"And then there is my mother who has an equal amount to my father, 30% each and then there is 20% by other investors. My father cannot decide to hire anyone to run this company who the board does not approve of.

"Apparently, my mother and siblings do not want the company to go into non-familial hands. To answer your question, that's why I am here."

Duke clenched his fist tightly; Travis could see the veins bulging at the side of his head. Maybe he had pushed him too far.

That thought was confirmed when Duke looked at him with cold murderous rage. "You are not going to win, all my life you win. Not this time brother."

"Stop being ridiculous," Travis said before Duke moved away, "when have I ever won, and you lost at something?"

Duke spun around. "Your very existence, my mother aborted five of your mother's children before you came. She tried to kill you, but you came anyway. A healthy boy. Before she died, she confessed that to me."

"You are special," she said. "That Travis is a winner, God-blessed, a survivor. She cried when she heard you were in that accident." Duke snorted. "I laughed. It couldn't have worked out better."

Travis winced at the malice that was practically exuding from Duke. "I know that you have been trying to undermine me all of my life."

Duke snorted. "Not all of your life. Just since I found out that you were my brother and I was never going to get the same privileges and recognition that you get. Then I began to resent you and your whole family."

"You had the same privileges as we did," Travis said, "you just didn't have the name."

Duke laughed harshly. "Really? The same privileges? When I was ten years old, I was taken from the only home I ever knew and lived in the ghetto for two whole years. My mother had to whore herself out for a full year to feed us before Miguel even looked at us."

"Miguel was broke. His business was going down. A rogue accountant stole all his money," Travis said tiredly. "All of your hate is misguided. My grandfather was the one who bailed him out. Without him, there would have been no Jefferson Pharmaceuticals or house in the hills or family wealth to be jealous over.

"You hate because you do not know the full story. It's easy to blame your sucky childhood on me, but I had as much of my father as you did back then."

Duke flinched. "You are deluded if you think that. I had nothing of Miguel. He could have acknowledged me. He could have made me feel wanted."

"Have you met the man?" Travis asked incredulously, "you have to hit him over the head when it comes to the finer feelings. I am crippled, and I could count the number of times my father voluntarily called me in ten years. He is not the father that you are looking for. You, running this company would not have miraculously changed Miguel Jefferson into something he is not."

"You talk like this because you have not lived my life," Duke said bitterly.

He walked out of the office and closed the door with controlled hostility. It was louder than a slam in Travis' ears.

Travis shuddered involuntarily at all the malevolence that was left behind. It felt like a physical thing. His phone rang almost at the same time.

He glanced at the display. It was an outside call. He hoped it wasn't Winston's mother calling to give him an earful. He had about as much as he could take today.

He answered briskly with a no-nonsense tone. It was his mother. He slumped at the desk.

"The planning for your father's birthday bash is coming along great," Pasha said brightly, "I have one teeny-weeny favor to ask of you."

"Mom, this is not the right time to be talking about parties," Travis said tiredly.

"I know you are at work," she said smugly, "I just want your advice on which three members of the press to invite. Just three."

Travis rubbed his hand over his face. "I only know one, Kenton Perkins. He deserves a scoop like this. He is the one who suggested to me that Duke was my brother."

"Oh," Pasha said dismissively.

"When exactly did you know?" Travis asked.

"About what?"

"About Duke."

"From the moment he was born," Pasha said grimly, "and I allowed Arlene to continue living at the house for ten years after that. I only let her go after she confessed something too dark for me to repeat."

The miscarriages. Travis didn't push her to elaborate. "Duke is bitter about his whole growing up years," he said instead. "I think you, dad and Arlene created a monster."

Pasha snorted. "Don't blame me, blame your dad. If he had come out right and told me about Duke years ago, I would have treated that boy like family. But that's all water under the bridge now."

"I'll invite Kenton Perkins and two other persons. Have a good day, honey." Pasha hung up the phone.

Travis put his head in his hands. He had too many things to process. Too many thoughts and regrets swimming around in his mind. He opted to have lunch with Sky. She could distract him.

****

"Let us play that time travel game," Travis said to Sky as she hungrily bit into her tuna melt sandwich. She bought lunch for the two of them from an eatery across the road. She insisted that he tried their tuna melt sandwich.

"It's not a game," Sky mumbled with her mouth full. "You are a resetter. You can reset the events in your life. You read the book and did your own research."

"So I did. But I still think it's a fantastic tale."

Sky grinned at him. "Okay, Mr. Skeptic."

"If I go back, where would I go?" Travis ignored his food. Sky looked at him without speaking.

"Come on, play along." Travis urged.

"You meant 'when' would you go. You would go back to the time that Milly met Ramone." Sky took another bite of her sandwich. "You could prevent her from being a junky."

"No, that's too late that was '82." Travis shook his head. "I was seventeen then, Milly twenty-two."

"You would go back to when you met evil Melanie." Sky grinned. "Tell her she is ugly as sin and destroy her self-confidence forever."

Travis chuckled. "That's still too late. I first met Melanie in '84 two years before the accident. I think I would go back to '75 that was the year that I was ten. Duke was nine. He was my very best friend in the whole world, Arlene was still at the house, my dad was a relatively good dad, and Munro, the accountant, hadn't run away with the money. Jefferson Pharmaceuticals was still in the black."

"Bob Marley was still alive," Sky said dreamily. "Tell him that he needs to get cancer treatment before it is too late."

Travis nodded. "Sure. I will tell him."

"I am serious." Sky wiped her lips with a napkin. "It would be nice to hear new music from him now."

"I'd be ten Sky," Travis picked up his sandwich. "Why would the reggae superstar listen to me, a kid? Besides, in 75 he was busy, that was the year the Jackson 5 came to Jamaica, and they performed together."

"Cool." Sky's eyes lit up. "Did you go to the concert?"

"No." Travis shook his head. "My mom and Dad did. I remember that time so vividly."

"I wasn't born yet." Sky chuckled.

Travis' eyes darkened. "If I go back, I am going to have to wait until you grow up."

"Yes, please." Sky nodded," don't you dare forget me. And don't fool around with anybody else."

Travis laughed. "In other words be a monk, when all my parts would be working?"

"Uhm... yes." Sky chuckled. "Be a monk until I grow up. At the very least do not fall in love with anyone."

"That's doable. I never fell in love with anyone until you." Travis steepled his fingers. "So when should I approach you?"

"When I am done with Mount Faith." Sky clipped her fingers, "no, when I am done with the masters. I'll be twenty-three then. It's a good age to get married. Don't you think?

"Sure." Travis nodded solemnly.

"You will have to romance me all over again." Sky grinned, "I feel sorry for you. You will have to convince me that we knew each other in another timeline, and what if I fall in love with someone else by then."

Travis frowned. "Not going to happen."

"I might." Sky giggled, "and you are going to have to convince me that we knew each other and that I should give up my current love for you."

Travis chuckled. "That sounds like a task. We wouldn't have anything in common anymore if I go back. You'd be a student. I would be...I don't know, if I go back I definitely won't be in a wheelchair, at least not from that jet ski crash and I wouldn't be a lecturer at Mount Faith. That's for sure. I'd probably be here running the company."

Sky grimaced. "Way out of my league. I'd probably see you on television and go, what a handsome dude."

"Tell me something, if I go back to this pathway and think about the time that I need to go back to, how do I explain being in Manchester and how would I get back home to Kingston?"

"That's easy," Sky said. "That place would be an empty lot. My father and uncle didn't build there until the '80s, but Gwendolyn Fisher Campbell would still be alive. You would have to go up to her place and have her call your parents. Wait a minute, did they have phones in Jamaica in 75?"

"Yes, they did." Travis raised an eyebrow at her and shook his head. "My father had one at the house."

"Try and remember the phone number." Sky warned. "Then have an adult call them, and then they can come pick you up. Of course, you would have to explain to them why you were in Mandeville."

Travis laughed. "I love this game. I know things will never happen this way, but it is so good to fantasize."

"One day, something will happen that will make you do it." Sky took a sip of her drink. "Something will happen that will make you think you absolutely have to change things and then you'll be grateful that you had a plan."

Chapter Fifteen

June 1996

The Jefferson's mansion was alight with colorful pepper lights. There was a steel band playing by the poolside. The front door was opened wide, and you could see all the way to the poolside and the view of twinkling city lights beyond. It felt like a magical night for Sky. This was her first time coming to a party like this. She was dressed in designer wear that Travis had insisted on and made up so smartly that when June was done with her, she hadn't recognized herself in the mirror.

And all of this was for Miguel Jefferson who was seventy today, Sunday, June 2, 1996.

"I didn't want to come," Milly complained beside Sky. She was dressed in a long-sleeved black dress, which hid the track scars on her arms. June had done her makeup too. It did Milly a world of good, hiding her pockmarks and blemishes.

Her sparse hair was under a long brown wig. She looked like a different person as well. June was a genius.

Sky had told her that many times this evening.

"You look good though." Sky complimented Milly.

"I look okay, you look good," Milly said cracking a rare smile. "My brother gasped when you walked out into the living room tonight."

"Come on," Travis rolled up to them, "what are you two talking about?"

"How good Sky looks," Milly said taking a step toward the door and then grimacing, "I can't wear these heels, not even for my father." She took them off and headed toward the door with them in hand.

"You do look good, better than good," Travis said looking up at her. "Come here."

Sky leaned down to him, and he kissed her. "Now, when the men here approach you tonight what are you going to tell them?"

"That I am taken by the most handsome disabled guy in the room." Sky laughed.

"And?" Travis caressed her face.

"And I love him like no other, and I would not countenance leaving him for anyone in the whole wide world."

Travis released her. "Good, you know I love you, don't you?"

"Yes." Sky grinned at him. "I love you always forever, near and far... I will be with you, everywhere I will be with you, everything I will do for you...

"Now you have that song playing in my head," Travis grumbled, and with reason, she had the song blasting every morning before work.

"Come on, it's a nice romantic song." Sky laughed. "It is my song of the year."

When she and Travis entered the hallway with its sparkling chandelier and easily recognizable faces, his mother floated toward them in an off-white sari in gold trimmings.

"Honey you made it." She greeted Travis and then Sky profusely.

"I hope you guys enjoy the party." She was on to the next guest.

"It didn't take them long before they were joined by a few persons who Travis identified as family and they had a little chit-chat.

Sky was enjoying the atmosphere of the party. The steel band was belting out smooth melodies that made her sway to the music. Sky spotted Betsy who introduced her to her husband. He was a doctor who wore horn-rimmed glasses. The toasts and well wishes followed then Miguel Jefferson took center stage.

He was dressed in a tux. He looked very young for his age.

"Three score and ten," he said solemnly into the mike. "This is a milestone is it not, a very significant number Biblically, that was the time apportioned to man. And yet here I am, still feeling relatively healthy, except for a little headache now and again I haven't been sick in years."

"You run a pharmaceutical company," somebody mocked at the front.

Miguel laughed. "And there is that. My products work!" His guests chuckled. "Anyway, since this is a milestone birthday, I am about to do something I have never done before. "

The place was still when he said that.

"I would like my wife, my ex-wife, my children, and grandchildren to come up here."

Sky looked at Travis. He was sitting close to her. She squeezed his hand before he made his way over to the platform area.

Sky had never seen Marla before. She was a white lady with heavily tanned skin and blue eyes, tall and willowy. Her daughter, Carly, resembled her quite a bit. Elizabeth looked like a combination of both her parents' genes. And Milly, well, she looked older than her mother.

"They are all here," Miguel said when his family gathered on the stage looking like mini united nations.

"All except one," Sky whispered to herself. She looked in the crowd to see if Duke was lurking nearby and she saw him standing at the back with his arms folded, no expression on his face.

That must hurt. Sky thought looking back to the front.

Miguel was looking at his family. "I have never said this before, but I am sorry. I could have been a better husband, a better father, a better friend. Some people might think that it is too late now, but I want to be a better person.

"I want to be the kind of person who... "

He continued talking, but Sky was distracted. There was a sinister looking guy dressed all in black who was pushing his way from the back of the crowd and heading to the front. He had a gun.

The minute that thought registered, she froze and then she was pushing to the front too, without thought, her heart drumming in her ears.

Gun! She thought she screamed it, but she didn't.

She saw when his hands went up. He was aiming for Travis.

"Gun!" She finally found the voice to scream. "Gun!"

She was running toward the stage as pandemonium erupted around them.

Then there was one shot fired, then another. She could feel the explosion from the blast; the sound was heavy in her ears.

The gunman was shooting at the family in the front who were at the mercy of his shots. She lunged right before Travis and then her legs went weightless.

****

Travis looked in horror as Milly who was just standing to the right of him fell in a loud explosion and then his nephew to his right.

The gunman wasn't masked; it was Rocky from the three R's. This was an older version of Rocky with wild eyes.

His aim had been off. He was almost sure that Rocky was there to kill him.

Weirdly, it all made sense. Duke had said he would eliminate Travis. Surely Duke didn't think he could get away with this?

The links were too obvious.

He was staring death in the face, and all he could think of was that Duke would kill his entire family.

Don't do it, Rocky, Travis thought sickly, "Stop now."

And then miraculously in a split second, he couldn't see Rocky's bloodshot eyes or his trembling black tipped fingers because Sky had jumped in the way.

And twice, the gun went off.

He heard when the shot connected with her body and saw when she sunk to the ground in a heap. The security reached Rocky's side and tackled him to the ground at the same time.

"Sky!" Travis wheeled as fast he could move to her side. Blood was already pooling around her head.

"Sky!" Travis' voice was a hoarse croak. She wasn't moving. He locked the chair and fell to the ground crawling toward her body; he cradled her head not caring that her blood was all over him.

"Sky!" she was limp and lifeless.

Chapter Sixteen

It didn't take the police long to reach the residence. Nobody could pry Travis away from Sky. He sat there with her cradled in his arms for what seemed like an eternity.

He heard talking and sobbing. He didn't know if some of the sobbing wasn't his. His ears were blocked from the explosions.

"Travis," a large hand finally rested on his shoulders, and he recognized Kenton's voice. Kenton Perkins the reporter, Amelia's brother. It was amazing how he could process those details.

"Travis, the police want to process the crime scene."

Kenton had tears in his eyes, and Travis wondered why he was crying.

"Can you do something for me?" Travis whispered hoarsely.

"Anything." Kenton nodded.

"Take me to Mandeville."

"What?" Kenton looked confused.

"To Sky's house. I need to go there."

"The police will call her family, honey." It was his mother's voice to his right.

Travis inhaled shakily. "If you take me to Mandeville right now, I'll make it worth your while Kenton. I promise."

Kenton stood up and stretched to his greatest height. "Okay."

"No, he can't leave." His mother protested. "He needs to wash all that blood off himself."

"I need to go now." Travis was firm. "Can my chair hold in your van?"

"Sure." Kenton nodded.

They helped him in his chair.

He looked around. There was debris everywhere. Milly's shoes were near the wheels of his chair. She was lying right where she fell. Paramedics were nursing his nephew, Brenton; at least he was alive, covered in blood but still breathing.

There were flashing lights from sirens outside. His mother looked bewildered as if she wasn't quite sure that she was awake or dreaming. His father now looked every bit of his seventy years. He was talking to a detective bewilderment in his voice in his expression.

And then there was Sky.

Lifeless. Dead. His Sky. She had taken two bullets for him. He had to see if all this talk of time traveling was worth it because he could never live with himself after this. He couldn't return to his apartment after this. Life could not just go on after this.

Kenton helped him in the van. He looked grim.

"You do know that this is very strange don't you?" Kenton asked him when they were driving downhill.

"I know." Travis nodded. "I would drive myself, but I don't think my hands are steady enough to handle a vehicle."

"So why are we going to Sky's house in Mandeville?" Kenton asked.

"Because I am going to make sure that none of this happens." Travis inhaled ruggedly.

"You are not thinking straight," Kenton said calmly. "How can you make sure that this never happens?"

"By resetting it." Travis held up his bloodstained hands. "I only have two lines in my palms. I am a resetter. I am going back."

"This is madness," Kenton whispered under his breath. "Just so you know I am only doing this because I know you told your mother to invite me to the party. I appreciate that."

"Thank you. " Travis closed his eyes and clenched his teeth. He never wanted to see those images in his head again.

"Have you always wanted to be a journalist?" Travis asked when they were on their way, the roads were clear at this time of the night, and he needed to stop the night's events from replaying in his head.

"Yes." Kenton nodded, "I would love to work in television. Always been my dream to be a news producer and maybe do other news shows."

Travis inhaled. "Okay, when I go back I'll make it happen for you."

Kenton glanced at him and then shook his head. "You know you are a little bit crazy."

"Just a little is all it takes," Travis said cryptically.

****

It was two o'clock in the morning when they reached Sky's house. The backlights were on in both houses. There was no movement at either place. Travis remembered Sky telling him that her aunt and uncle had gone to the States for the summer.

Travis directed Kenton to drive as close to the stone as possible. He could see the blue stone all he needed to do was get to it. The blood had long dried on his tuxedo shirt. He didn't care.

"What if someone is home and gets out and shoots us?" Kenton helped him into his chair.

"Then that would be tragic," Travis said, his voice sounded croaky.

"What are you going to do now?" Kenton whispered fearfully.

"I am going back to June 1, 1975." Travis inhaled. "My parents went to the airport to pick up my grandfather that day. I could probably get home before they do."

Kenton was frowning at him. "Maybe I should call for help?"

Travis wheeled toward the stone. "Give me a few minutes, before you do." He placed his palm on the blue rock; there was already an imprint of a palm on it. He closed his eyes. The rock became warmer and gave him a zing in his open palm. And then he felt a falling down the tunnel kind of feeling.

It didn't work!

He opened his eyes and was about to confess to Kenton that yes, he needed medical attention that the shock from the shooting had him believing a myth, but there was no Kenton. There were no houses.

There was bright sunlight where there was only night before his head was in line with the lowest part of the rock. He took a tentative step toward the open lot and realized that he could walk. He could walk!

He started running around. It worked!

Chapter Seventeen

Open lot. Blue skies. He took stock of his environment. There were open lots as far as his eyes could see. There were no structures around. The house on the hill was the lone structure in the vicinity. He looked down at himself he was in church wear.

So it was Sunday. Was it 1975?

He couldn't quite believe this was happening; just a few moments ago he witnessed Sky's death.

Now, he was what, ten? Was this June 1?

He walked up the hill to the house. When he had come here before, in 1996, there were yesterday, today and tomorrow flowers planted along the winding driveway in full bloom. Now they were just seedlings.

His footsteps slowed the closer he got to the house. Would anyone in there believe him?

The door was closed.

He went right up to it and knocked. In 1975 there was no

grillwork around the edifice.

"Coming," he heard a lady's voice say. "Hold on a minute."

He stepped back from the door and waited, looking over at the green landscape.

And then the door was opened, and a lady answered the door. She had a pleasant round face and dimples in her cheeks.

She smiled at him. "May I help you?"

"Yes er..." Travis paused in his speech. His voice sounded so childlike.

The lady waited on him.

"Are you Miss er Mrs. Gwen Fisher Campbell?"

"Oh yes," she smiled. "You are in the right place if you are looking for me. Everyone calls me Miss Gwen, dear."

"I ah. I don't know how to tell you this," Travis cleared his throat, it was taking him a while to get used to this squeaky little boy voice of his. "But I am a resetter; I am coming from the year 1996."

Miss Gwen leaned on the door in astonishment. "A resetter? Good heavens."

"Come on have a seat." She gestured to the chair on the verandah.

Travis was about to protest he had been sitting in a wheelchair for ten years it was nice to be on his feet, but he sat down as she had indicated.

"I don't know where to start." Miss Gwen was looking him over thoroughly, "'96 you would have been what?"

"Thirty-one," Travis said his voice squeaky.

"Oh but..." Miss Gwen still looked shocked. "You are a baby now!"

"I had to come back to now and stop bad things from happening. I think I have to start by resetting my family." He swallowed when he thought of Sky lying lifeless on the floor. "I have to make sure some things never happen."

"Ah," Miss Gwen was nodding, "I see."

"I also read your diary." Travis inhaled shakily, "the one where you and your husband Vernon went to Oswald King's house after Frederick died from typhoid fever."

Miss Gwen gasped. "I just wrote that yesterday! How did you get it? Are we related?"

Travis smiled. "I know. I saw the date. Monica gave your diary to Skyler's cousin Addison who is also a resetter. They will be living down at the land with the blue stone."

"I wasn't going to sell that land." Miss Gwen frowned. "It has a pathway it has to be kept in the family."

"You sold it to the Porters," Travis said, "The girls I am talking about aren't even born yet."

"Oh heavens," Miss Gwen repeated. "One of them is a resetter? What's her name?"

"Her name is Addison Porter."

"Good heavens." Miss Gwen whispered again.

"Grandma, everything all right?" A young Monica looked out at them through the window.

"Yes dear." Miss Gwen grunted. "Good heavens."

Monica came out on the veranda and looked at Travis. "Who are you?"

Travis stared at her for a long while and then smiled. She looked pretty much the same when he had met her in 1996. She was just younger and slimmer now.

Monica frowned at him. "Why are you distressing my grandmother?"

"I am not distressing her, Monica," Travis said, "We are just talking."

"You know my name?" Monica asked.

Miss Gwen was rocking back and forth and muttering, 'good heavens'.

The fact that he was a resetter was still sinking in for her.

"Where is Vernon?" Travis asked as Monica folded her arms and glared at him.

"Mr. Campbell to you," Monica hissed, "he died last year from a brain aneurysm."

"It runs in his family." Miss Gwen focused on Travis and sighed. "That's why I couldn't go back to save him. It might have happened to him earlier. It might have happened later. There wasn't anything my resetting could do except give me more grief. I would have still lost him."

"Sorry about your loss, Miss Gwen," Travis said feelingly. "I know how much you loved him from reading your diaries."

"My grandmother does not have any diaries," Monica growled. "Who is this little boy, grandma?"

"You know Monica from the future?" Miss Gwen whispered.

"Yes," Travis nodded, "she is my girlfriend's..."

"No," Miss Gwen shook her head. "Let it be how it is supposed to be. No foreknowledge you have said enough."

Monica glowered at him, "What are you talking about?"

"I haven't told her yet." Miss Gwen smiled at Travis. "Thought I would do so soon. She is the only one, except for her father Burt who would believe me."

Travis nodded. "She will believe you. She is your greatest believer."

"Who is this boy?" Monica screeched the question, obviously resenting the fact that they were talking mysteriously and ignoring her.

"A friend." Miss Gwen said getting up. "What is your name, son?" Miss Gwen asked belatedly.

"Travis, Miss Gwen. What date is this?"

"June 1, 1975." Monica was the one who answered. "How comes you are granny's friend, and she doesn't know your name? And how comes you don't know the date?"

Miss Gwen ignored Monica. "Where are you from, son?"

"I am from Kingston," Travis said softly. "My parent's don't know I am here."

"Good heavens," Miss Gwen muttered again.

****

Miss Gwen got Burt to drive him to Kingston. Burt was a police officer who worked in Spanish Town. He went there every Sunday. His car was a new Ford Escort, which Burt seemed to take great pride in and he blasted the radio all the way to Kingston while he chewed on gum. He didn't ask Travis any questions or directed any conversation to him.

When he drove up to the house, it was three o'clock in the evening; his parents and grandfather were standing at the front of the yard talking to two police officers.

His mother was sobbing when he got out.

"Where were you? Who is this? "

Travis did not get a chance to answer before his mother who seemed considerably taller than he remembered was folding him in a hug and running her fingers through his hair.

"We sent you to church with Arlene, where did you disappear to?" His father sounded pissed.

His father had an Afro and was wearing tight pants and platform shoes.

Travis bit back an effort to laugh. They looked just like that old photos that they had on the mantle place in the living room from the future. It was interesting to see his father looking so young, and his mother so rail thin.

"I brought him back from Mandeville." Burt was the one to reassure them. "My mother said he was her friend."

"Your mother? Friend? Mandeville?"

The questions were fast and incredulous.

The policemen recognized Burt. One of them was a batchmate of his. They directed their attention to Burt quite quickly, shaking hands with him and nodding in familiarity.

The batch mate started an unrelated conversation with Burt leaving the other policeman to reassure his bewildered parents that if he was in Burt's care, then it was okay.

They soon left. He only had his parents to face.

Travis sighed as he looked into his mother's tear-stained face and the worry lines on his father's, he couldn't read his grandfather's expression. It was neutral.

Chapter Eighteen

"**W**here were you, Travis Jefferson?" Pasha was in fine form.

His explanation that he time traveled from 1996 was holding no weight with her.

"You can't just run off. You can't just disappear from church." Pasha sobbed, she was more distressed than Travis had ever seen her, even when he had met in that accident that left him paralyzed.

The accident that wasn't going to happen.

"Give the boy some time to clean up and then have some dinner." His father was the voice of reason.

Travis stood in front of the stairs; he had not entered the top floor of this house for ages.

Not ages. He was just ten. He reminded himself wryly. He went to his room, which was neat as usual. Arlene was not allowed to clean it; his mother inspected it every week to make sure that he kept it clean.

Cleanliness was next to godliness, and she had been determined that he would be a neat boy.

He had his marbles and spin tops and his other little games tucked into a drawer, and his trucks and toy wagons stashed in the closet.

He reacquainted himself with his ten-year-old life quite quickly. He hadn't been a complicated boy. Besides, he had no time to dwell. He was starving.

He washed, luxuriating in the fact that he could just walk into the bathroom and get his ablutions done in record time. His mother always checked behind his ears. He cleaned there thoroughly, dressed in shorts and t-shirt and ran downstairs.

His parents and grandfather were already sitting at the formal dining table. Arlene was in the kitchen.

"Where were you, Travis Jefferson?"

Travis shook his head, "You wouldn't believe me."

"Good lord you almost gave everybody gray hair," Arlene muttered. "I couldn't find you after church. You want to eat in here with Duke?"

Arlene asked him. She was shaking her head as he walked around the kitchen looking around it in awe. His mother had renovated it in the mid-eighties. The country-style décor that it was now in, with its white cupboards and rooster tiles as the backsplash, were replaced with clean, modern lines.

"I ah, I have to eat with grandpa this evening," Travis answered after he looked around the space.

"Oh yes, your grandfather." Arlene responded, "very nice man. He brought me a watch from Canada as a present. Just in time too, my old watch is dead."

"Travis!" Duke skipped into the kitchen, he was a little shorter than he was and he had a bandage on his knee, and his ears looked a bit too big for his head. It was something that he had outgrown, and Travis had completely forgotten about.

His front tooth was just growing back; he looked like an innocent little boy without a care in this life.

He spoke with a slight lisp because of his teeth. "We are playing long remembrance when we are done eating, okay. I got a new set of cards."

"Okay." Travis smiled at him. "Sure."

He almost hugged him and said something inane like, "I am so happy to see you still so innocent and unspoiled. I am going to make sure that you never grow up to be a murderer."

Instead, he knocked knuckles with him and headed to the dining room.

****

Travis found himself wolfing down the traditional Sunday dinner of fried chicken, rice and peas, vegetables and candied sweet potatoes like a person who was starving for days. He had forgotten what a good cook Arlene was and how acute his ten-year-old taste buds were.

The taste of the food exploded on his tongue. All of it was homegrown. The chicken, vegetables, and peas were from his cousin Murphy's farm. The sweet potato he could vaguely recall was planted where the swimming pool would be in the future.

His mother watched him as he gobbled down the two plates of food and didn't say a word.

His father sternly told him no dessert when he was done with the second helping.

Travis nodded. "That is a fair punishment."

Miguel laughed aloud. "Say what? That's not your punishment. You waltz in here from Mandeville, you tell us some ridiculous explanation of how you reached there, and you expect that not having dessert is your punishment. You must think you are a spoiled rich kid."

Travis groaned and put his hand on his head.

He watched as Arlene served dessert, which was carrot cake with frosting and vanilla ice cream.

He was too full to be overly envious, but he found himself licking his lips as Arlene put down the last plate in front of his mother.

He cleared his throat and asked her. "Arlene, could you stay a while?"

She paused. The whole table froze. Apparently, this was an unusual request from ten-year-old Travis. Travis couldn't remember being assertive at ten, so yes this was a memorable moment.

He squared his shoulders and sat up straighter in the chair. He was not letting this opportunity pass.

His family was going to listen, and he was going to make them believe. He had a lot of arsenal at his disposal. The people here, his mom, dad, and Arlene had a few secrets that only they could know.

"I want to talk to the adults. Is Duke still eating?" He asked so solemnly that he got an automatic nod from Arlene.

His father protested. "What is this, boy? You calling conferences now?"

Travis inhaled. "Dad, Grandpa, Mom, Arlene...I really am coming from the future. In a couple of days, I will explain the why's and how's of it, but I want you to hear me out properly and take me very seriously.

"Dad," he looked at his father who had a slack-jawed look, they all did.

He guessed that they had never had a ten-year-old talk to them so firmly before. This was the '70s children were usually seen and not heard at least from what he could remember. He had to take advantage of the lapse.

"Dad," he repeated again, "Munro is a crook, he is funneling off your money in little increments to an offshore account. Tomorrow first thing when you go to work have AJ Sullivan, take over the accounts department. Audit Munro. If you don't do it, you will be staring down the uncomfortable barrel of poverty.

Miguel shook his head. "What?"

"You heard me." Travis wasn't mincing words, and he didn't have the luxury of time to make this easier. Besides, the quickest way to get his father to take him seriously was to talk about his money.

"First thing tomorrow, do not delay. AJ has been at you about auditing the books, listen to him."

"That's true, AJ has been on my case for a while." His father slapped the table. "Boy, how do you know this?"

"Because I am coming from '96." Travis turned to his mother who had a fearful look in her eyes as if she expected him to blurt out something else distasteful.

"Mom," He wasn't going to sugarcoat this revelation, "Duke is Dad's son."

Arlene gasped and was swaying on her feet like she didn't know if she should faint or stand still and hear more.

"You all know this," Travis said sternly, "especially you mom. You cannot continue to pretend that he is not Dad's son. You all need to deal with this before that innocent boy in the kitchen turns into a hate-filled murderer.

"He will if you ignore him and treat him like he is not yours. All he has ever wanted is his rightful place in this family. Like that poem you have hung up on the kitchen wall by Dorothy Law Nolte, if a child lives with acceptance he learns to love.

"That little boy in the kitchen needs to learn to love. My

suggestion to you Dad is to acknowledge him and call him a Jefferson openly. Make him matter, or you will regret it. You will all regret it."

He said it more forcefully than he intended to. He even hit the table for emphasis.

Arlene did the cross sign and started babbling a prayer. His mother started fidgeting in her chair. His father's eyes couldn't bulge any wider.

"And Dad," Travis said tiredly. "You have to find a way to delegate more at the office. You have to spend more time with Carly, Elizabeth, and Milly. Especially Milly. She is a girl that needs her father's attention.

"If you continue to ignore Milly she will turn into a drugged up junky. Shortly after this, she will be seeking love everywhere. She will start getting it from very unsuitable men because she has never gotten it from you."

He inhaled. Everybody was deathly still. "All of this is more important than running a company and stocks and shares."

He fixed his gaze on Arlene. She had tears in her eyes.

"Do not confess what you did to her, confess to God because she will never forgive you and the whole course of your life will change if you do."

Arlene swallowed and nodded. At least she believed him. She knew exactly what he was talking about.

"And Arlene. Keep Duke away from Ramone, Rocky, and Reese. By '87 Ramone will be killed in a turf war. Rocky will cause mayhem and death in this family and Reese will be in prison for murder."

"They are Peaches boys, my cousin Peaches," Arlene stammered. "They are family. They are just little boys."

"They are little boys now, but they will grow to be dangerous men. This is the time to change the course of their lives. Do not allow Duke near them, not unless they are moved out of that environment and learn to become responsible citizens."

Travis turned to his father. "Dad, you need to help those boys. Those three will end up in a bad place if you don't help them."

"How the hell do you know any of this?" Miguel grunted in disbelief. "How on God's green earth can you know this?"

"It doesn't matter how." Travis exhaled. "It matters that I do. I am here to change our future for the better, and you are going to all listen and take heed. I can't allow Sky to die."

"Who is Sky?" His grandfather spoke for the first time.

"My friend...my girlfriend...the woman I love," Travis said, realizing at the same time how weird what he was saying sounded. He was ten years old. He was talking about the woman that he loved to his grandfather.

"I watched her die before me on Dad's 70th birthday right over there he pointed to where the pool would be. I am not living through that again. I am not living through any of that again.

"The change starts here, around this table; the change starts with each of you. You all better make it happen. You have a responsibility to the children in your lives, whether they are yours or not, whether they are legitimate or not."

Maybe he shouldn't have said that. His father flinched. His mother looked at Arlene wide-eyed. He could feel the tension in the room.

"Go to your room." His father's voice was weak and trembly sounding. "You have given us more than enough counsel for the evening. The adults need to take it from here."

It was no use protesting that he was an adult too. Travis asked instead, "Can I go and play with Duke?"

"Yes. Go." His mother nodded.

"Arlene sit down," was the last thing that Trevor heard his

mother say.

****

He wasn't punished that night. They forgot to punish him, or they couldn't in all good conscience do so. He had after all; set them on the right path with his little speech.

His grandfather spent two weeks in Jamaica and most of that time he spent with Travis, asking him loads of questions about resetters. He found Oswald King's articles for himself at the library and drilled Travis about it.

"I am not around in '96 am I?" His grandfather asked him when he was leaving for Canada where he was currently residing.

"No." Travis shook his head. "That is why I had no counsel for you."

"It's my heart isn't it?"

"Yes," Travis nodded. "There was nothing that could be done about it. Maybe if you eat right and exercise and..."

"Pah, I know the drill. At least now the news won't be any surprise," his grandfather said wryly.

His grandfather squeezed his hand in the airport lounge. "Will I see you again?"

"Yes," Travis nodded, "for at least another couple more years."

He smiled at that. "Well, then I won't have to rush home to my lawyers to adjust my will. You deserve a special thank you, my special grandchild."

"Grandpa," Travis held his hands, "you don't have to."

"Oh yes, I do." His grandfather winked at him before going off to the departure lounge.

****

It had been a turbulent few weeks in his family; his father took Travis' advice about Munro. He had the accounting department taken over and audited the very next day. Munro had already funneled millions out of the company account with his creative accounting. By the end of the month, the police arrested him at home. He had to pay back every single dollar.

July was not allowed to run its course before his father hired vice presidents who were in charge of key departments.

The accounting system had more checks and balances than before, and his father spent more time with his children.

Late July, family time became a staple in the Jefferson household. At their very first meeting, the announcement was made that Duke's name was changed on his birth certificate.

He was officially and proudly a Jefferson and Miguel's favorite golf pal. Travis never cared much for the game. He didn't begrudge them the time they spent together bonding either.

In August, Travis spent a lot of time with his dad in the office. He told him about future trends; he created policies for the company that was way ahead of the time.

Miguel's staff found it odd that their president had his ten-year-old son with mounds and mounds of paperwork before him and that he took advice from him even when they sounded a bit off.

"Do you have to go to school in September?" Miguel asked him in late August.

"I guess so," Travis grinned, "that's what ten-year-olds do."

"And when will you lose the memories of before?" Miguel asked concerned.

"They are already fading, Dad." He looked at Miguel sympathetically; Miguel had come to depend more and more on him as the weeks went by especially as it related to how he treated his children.

"You have more information to be the leader in the market for several years to come, and the girls are warming up to you. You are turning into a father to be proud of. You are getting there."

Miguel nodded. Tears pooling in the corner of his eyes. "Thank you." He blinked them away. "Oh, I forgot to show you something."

He held up a framed poem. "Your mother gave me this for my birthday the night after you surprised us with your speech. She said that when you quoted a line from it and mentioned that it hung in the kitchen, she was sure that you were telling the truth about the future because she hadn't given it to me yet. It was sitting in the room just waiting to be delivered. I guess it was her way to rebuke me for my unfatherly like qualities.

She got this one made for the office. The one you mentioned was put in the kitchen today so that you can memorize again when you revert to your ten-year-old mind."

Travis grinned. "Imagine that, I just remembered that it was there. Didn't remember when it was put there."

****

Home life was vastly different from before. Arlene was treating him with a quiet reverence. She had taken to making only the things that he liked for dinner.

Miguel had to warn her to stop telling her friends and anyone who would listen that Travis was spirited away from church one Sunday and that the Lord showed him the future and he was back to make it right for everyone. That was her testimony in church for eight straight Sundays.

She had random strangers showing up at the house to see Travis to tell them their futures and what God had planned for them. It got so bad that Travis had taken to hiding out when he saw one of Arlene's church members.

For Arlene, the spiriting-away was easier to swallow than the whole resetting business.

And then one day in the kitchen, Arlene looked at him and asked, "Travis, what am I doing in '96. Am I still a helper to your parents? Did I find a good Christian man to marry and have more children?"

Travis stiffened and then turned to her. "No, you are not around in '96."

"I am dead," Arlene whispered. "How?"

"Cancer," Travis said it softly. "Breast cancer. You were diagnosed with it in '82. You ignored it, and it spread. You will be dead by '85."

"For goodness sake." Arlene covered her mouth. "I am going to die, twelve years from now?"

"You don't have to die." Travis patted her arm. "Start taking measures to prevent it. Do regular checks. If it is caught early, there are things you can do."

Arlene looked at him with tears in her eyes. "Thank you for telling me. I mean it. Thank you for everything.

"You are welcome, Arlene." Travis sighed. "Your death made Duke even more of a bitter person."

Arlene nodded. "But now, he'll have you all, even your mother. I see her talking to him in her garden, showing him things, treating him right. It makes me feel so guilty.

"I was about to tell her you know when you told me two months ago not to. I was going to confess. I was bitter and jealous, and I thought that I had a chance with Miguel so I..."

Travis nodded solemnly. "I know."

"I know you told me not to confess to her, but I feel as if I need to tell her even if she sends me away. Some things just need to be out there." Arlene sniffed. "Travis, I am not the same woman who ground up papaya seeds and put in her food and her drinks so that she could miscarry. At first, I didn't even know it would work. I changed, Travis. I stopped lusting after Miguel a long, long time ago.

"We only slept together that one night, he was drunk after a party, your mother was pregnant with you and bedridden, and I thought that I deserved my chance with him. I know it was wrong. Maybe I deserve cancer. Maybe that is my punishment."

"Nobody deserves cancer." Pasha came fully into the room stunning both Travis and Arlene.

"Miss Pasha," Arlene was shocked and trembling. "I didn't mean...I...oh God." Arlene covered her face. "I am so sorry Miss Pasha. I am so sorry."

"I heard it all," Pasha said coldly. "And I am not going to send you away. We'll talk about this some other time."

At first, his mother and Arlene had a cold truce. By December, the coldness faded. Pasha was the one who gently nudged Arlene to start her own catering business because she had exceptional culinary skills. Jefferson Pharmaceuticals annual Christmas bash was her first outing.

She did so well after that that she couldn't handle her bookings. She trained her family and some friends to help with the business. The first person to benefit from the training was Peaches. She moved to midtown, to a safer area, and sent her boys to live with their grandparents in the country.

The three R's, Peaches boys, were never a significant part of their lives. Ramone was Spelling Bee champion for the island in '81, Rocky saved a younger boy from drowning, and it made the news.

The prime minister gave him an award for bravery. He wore it around his neck even to bed, and he liked it so much he decided to get more, he was the most helpful boy in his neighborhood. The most popular, well-loved, well- behaved child in Jamaica or that was how his mother told it.

He entered politics in 1986, the youngest MP to ever have his own constituency.

It was such a 180-degree turn from the Rocky who had stood at his father's party and killed Milly and Sky, that when Travis read back his accounts from the other timeline, he even started doubting himself.

And then there was Reese, the artist. He opted to go to Edna Manley School of the Visual Arts. One of his paintings got the attention of Air Jamaica. They featured him in their annual calendar, and he became a sought-after member of the art world.

****

By 1980, Travis was in high school most of his memories of the life before had faded, most of them except those surrounding Skyler. He couldn't let her go. He didn't want to. He had painstakingly written down every moment about their time together.

The older he got, the more reading about her felt like he was reading about a dream, but he had a niggling sureness in the back of his mind that she was the one for him.

He drew pictures of her, he wrote down her description and had a professional artist paint her. The guy did such a good job he had him paint her in several settings.

He had him paint her when they just met at Mount Faith, in his class. Studying in his apartment with the textbook on her belly, laughing at one of his jokes.

He wrote down every single detail about Sky that he could remember. She was not a memory that he was willing to lose, but other things he forgot.

His friendship with Winston Bayer never happened. They

were just acquaintances. Their parents were friends, and he worked at Jefferson Pharmaceuticals and for a brief while he was the man in Melanie Pitter, the supermodel's life.

He had a few best friends Duke was one of them. They spent most of their time together.

Duke lived with them after Arlene got married to an American and migrated in 1980. She fell madly in love with one of her customers when she catered for a function he was involved in. The feeling was mutual. By the end of 1980, Arlene was packing to live with her new husband.

Duke begged to stay behind.

As for Milly, it was clear that she had an addictive personality, but instead of drugs, she was addicted to defending the planet. It was her passion. She became an environmentalist and an activist fighting for animal rights and any other green earth initiatives.

She met Wayne Gonzales in 1984 a man who was just as passionate about the environment as she was. He was a former lawyer who had butted heads with the establishment far too many times and had had enough.

They married and lived on a farm in the Blue Mountains only coming out of their green reserve to demonstrate about some harm to the environment or to have dinner with the family.

Wednesday family night at the Jefferson's was still a thing. It had survived because Miguel was resolved that it would. He was determined to be a family man, and he excelled at it.

****

July 1995

As for Melanie, he never met her in the '80s. He saw her in magazines. Duke pointed her out one day while they were sitting at the poolside waiting for Sunday brunch to be ready. They both took the opportunity to return home for a meal on Sundays every chance they got.

"Look at this woman," Duke said shaking the page. "She is gorgeous."

Travis grinned. "You were married to her in the other timeline."

"Her?" Duke shook the magazine. "I was married to Melanie Pitter?"

Travis chuckled. "You weren't happy with her. She gets around, and she was sleeping with half the board at Jefferson Pharmaceutical."

Duke grimaced. "You sure about that?"

"Yes, well, I don't know. Milly was the one who told me so, but she was a junky at the time, so you never know."

"Milly? Our sister Milly?" Duke asked incredulously. "Green juice drinking, vegetarian Milly, who thinks you are an accessory to murder for eating chicken was a junkie?"

"Yep." Travis nodded. "I wrote it down."

"Well if you wrote it down," Duke said doubtfully. "My mother said you saved her from cancer in the '80s, she caught it very early and dealt with it promptly, that is the only reason why I keep on believing this resetting business."

"Don't be so skeptical," Travis chuckled.

"Hmmph." Duke snorted. "I don't know. This Melanie girl is hot."

Travis sighed and then clipped his fingers to get Duke's attention. "By the way, I didn't see you sign up for the mentorship program at the office."

"Do I have to?" Duke murmured.

"Yes. Those inner-city children need role models. You are very much suited for this kind of volunteer work."

Duke looked over at Travis and held up the magazine.

"Look at this, 'Jefferson Pharmaceutical the leading company for employees with disabilities.' Now I know why Dad had this publication just lying around."

Travis chuckled.

"Woah, hear this." Duke read. "Travis Jefferson, the chief operating officer at Jefferson Pharmaceuticals, is working hard to change the way that companies view disabled persons in Jamaica. He has no problems hiring and promoting people with disabilities, and he goes one step further. He urges his colleagues and business associates to create spaces in their companies for wheelchair access; this includes bathrooms and boardrooms and offices."

"Yep." Travis smiled. "I was disabled once. I'll never forget it."

Duke shook his head. "You were disabled, and you have an imaginary girlfriend."

"She is very much real." Travis rebutted. "I have a detective tracking her every move."

"Stalker," Duke grunted. "When are we going to meet her?"

"2000," Travis said, "That will give her enough time to finish her degrees."

"Crazy talk." Duke went back to his magazine. "Can we use Melanie Pitter for something? I want to meet her."

Chapter Nineteen

Miguel was sitting at the head of the sizeable twenty-seater dining room table. He knocked his glass to get everyone's attention.

"I would like to thank my wife, Pasha, for making this an intimate family occasion and not a big party with dozens of faces I wouldn't recognize. Except for Kenton Perkins, everyone here is family, and it does my heart good to see that. Kenton is always around, and I am beginning to think of him as family."

Kenton raised his glass and grinned. "You need friendly family media coverage, and yes I am family."

Miguel chuckled and raised his glass.

Travis was sitting across from Kenton. They grinned at each other. He had befriended Kenton years ago at university. To this day Kenton had no idea why Travis Jefferson had sought him out and had so entrenched himself in his life that they were the best of pals.

"I have been blessed." Miguel continued and cleared his throat, "Immensely blessed. Twenty-one years ago my life could have gone differently, but God sent a message to my son, Travis. The message was buckle up and be a man. I heeded. I realized that what was important was my family and our relationship, the way we treat each other and love each other."

"That wasn't quite what happened," Travis muttered, but he allowed his father to do his grandstanding.

"I love my family. All five of my children they have been a blessing to me. And the grandkids too, I love you all. And now I am about to announce my retirement. This is no secret; you all know I want to be able to play golf all day.

"I am stepping down as chairman of the board. As you know, I own 50% shares in the company each child owns 10%. I have discussed this with you individually, and we came to a decision that Travis should be chairman of the company. We all know he has been running the place for a long while anyway. I was just there to sign the documents."

There was laughter around the table.

"Duke will be the chief operating officer for the Caribbean. Carly is already in charge of the research division, and Elizabeth is our branding manager.

"I wouldn't be Miguel Jefferson if I didn't have a toast for Milly."

There was laughter again as Miguel looked at Milly fondly.

"To Milly, my untamed, defiant wild child, the only person who will go toe-to-toe with me in her passionate love for the earth. I know that though we do not see eye to eye that you love your old man."

"Yes I do," Tears were rolling down Milly's cheek

unchecked. "I love you, papa."

"And so, Pasha and I have discussed it. We will come to your farm this summer. We will live a strict natural life with you and Wayne and the grandchildren and see what the whole hoopla is about with this nature thing."

"That would be wonderful." Milly chuckled. "You won't regret your stay. Prepare to be amazed. Wayne and I would love to have you and Aunty Pasha."

Miguel groaned audibly.

Pasha nodded. "I am looking forward to it, dear."

"And before I sit, my birthday wish for my sons," Miguel said, "is that they both find someone to marry. I look forward to having grandbabies with my surname."

Travis covered his eyes.

Duke was grinning from ear to ear.

"Kenton do not write that in your article tomorrow," Duke warned looking across at Kenton.

Kenton shook his head. "This is not new news. He has said it in several interviews over the years."

"I second that sentiment, Miguel." Pasha declared holding up her glass.

"Here, here," the rest of the family said.

****

September 1996

"Here are your Skyler Porter pictures, boss." His detective Garfield handed him the brown envelope and sat across from him. It was Monday morning his usual face-to-face reporting time. Skyler had classes all day.

"She is doing well in school. Her life is boring as heck, and she broke up with the guy she was seeing last week."

Travis smiled at that. "Why? I thought you said she was head over heels."

"She was telling her ex-roommate Emma in the cafeteria that she felt like there was someone else in the world for her, but it wasn't Darren. That was his name. He was complaining that he hardly saw her. Apparently, she is too into her books."

"That's my girl." Travis whistled. "She still studying hard?"

"Yes. I hardly see her." Garfield scratched the side of his head. "Seems like that's all she does. She is a boring subject, to be honest. I can understand why that Darren guy left her."

"You not satisfied with your pay?" Travis raised a brow, "or accommodations? If not, I can get someone else."

"No, no, no," Garfield shook his head. "This is the best gig I have ever gotten. I mean when she went to Disney World with her family in May I had a lot of fun, though I was watching her. She is not that boring."

Travis nodded. "No, she isn't. She hasn't figured out who pays her scholarship has she?"

"No siree," Garfield shook his head. "She is doing both summer sessions."

"As she should. She'll graduate faster." Travis smiled satisfied. "So all is going swimmingly?"

Garfield nodded and stood up. "I have always wanted to ask, how did you know that her fridge wouldn't be working and how did you know that the repair guy would hit on her?"

"You warned him off before he hit on her didn't you?" Travis asked.

"Yeah, I did scared the bejeezus out of him." Garfield nodded. "One more thing, she has never met you has she?"

"No." Travis smiled. "She is finishing this degree first and then her masters, and then I get her back here where she belongs."

"But how do you even know her." Garfield sputtered. "How is it...?" He shook his head and then walked out of Travis' office. He never got an answer when he probed.

****

January 1997

Kenton called him when he was leaving the office. He wanted to do a session in the company gym, but Betty handed him the phone on the way out.

"Hey man, my sister, Amelia has been bugging me to introduce you to her. I am in the vicinity, and she is here with me. Do you want us to do dinner? Say seven o'clock?"

"Sure." Travis had always heard Kenton talk about Amelia. He knew she worked at Mount Faith University. He wondered if they had crossed paths in the other time. He had no record of her in any of his files.

"I am going to the gym. Want us to meet at the Pegasus?"

"Yes." Kenton sounded pleased, "see you there."

Travis picked up his gear and headed for the bank of elevators. He had not gone out on a date for close to a year. For years he felt like he was cheating on Sky if he had just looked at another woman.

Sky who he hadn't spoken to yet. Sky who didn't even know he existed.

Celibacy was something that was not as difficult for him to practice as he had thought it would be. In the last couple of years while he waited for Sky to come to him he had been ridiculously fastidious where sex was concerned.

The gym was his outlet these days, and he wondered not for the first time if it was still worth it. What was he waiting for?

He was lonely. He could drag Sky out of university convince her that they had a thing in an alternate timeline and wait for her to fall in love with him again or he could just move on with his life, take another direction.

It was time. The more he thought about his Sky stories from the other timeline, the more he was convinced that what he had with Sky before was half fantasy and half reality. Why would any young pretty co-ed be interested in a guy in a wheelchair?

And when they were together had she really loved him? Or was he fantasizing about that too?

And did she really throw herself into the line of fire for him and save his life or had she been running away and accidentally got caught in the shooter's crosshairs.

Were his writings even true? What if he had lied to himself? Penning about a fantasy woman that couldn't meet up to his present-day expectations. He had changed drastically from the man he was before. What if Sky was not the partner for him now? Maybe she had been perfect for wheelchair-bound Travis, the university lecturer, not Travis the CEO of a large corporation.

The whole situation was driving him crazy. He got on the treadmill and started walking at a brisk pace.

He had doubts every time Garfield visited these past couple of weeks, and now he was practically buried under an avalanche of them right now. He cranked up the speed of the treadmill and increased the incline.

Maybe he should fire Garfield, let Sky live her life, and he live his. If they were to meet again, then it would be a true sign that they should always meet.

He was doing his best by Sky. She had a full scholarship. He was working behind the scenes to make her future an unbelievably good one.

Maybe that was all he should do. Holding out for romance with her was probably a long shot. A dream that needed to be put to rest.

A dream that may never happen.

He wiped the sweat from his brow and reset the incline.

****

Amelia Perkins was surprisingly beautiful, as Kenton had said. Somehow Travis had doubted his claims that she was his sister.

She was definitely someone who you would take a second look at if you were driving by. She was petite and curvy and at their initial meeting had the kind of personality that was compatible with his.

She was witty and entertaining, and he found himself warming to her in a few seconds. Kenton excused himself to go to the office on what was obviously a made up errand to leave Travis alone with her. Travis didn't mind.

She was good company.

"So tell me," Amelia said flipping her hair over her shoulders in a gesture that managed to be sexy and casual at the same time.

"How is it that Travis Jefferson, the man in the prime of his life, the leader of one of the Caribbean's top companies is still single?"

Travis leaned back in his chair and shrugged. "It is the way it is for now."

He pictured Sky's half smile from a picture that Garfield had taken of her last week. And then closed his eyes briefly and focused on Amelia who was chuckling at his answer.

"Or you work too hard?"

"I do work hard," Travis shrugged, "but there is a balance. I get that there is time for family. I learned that from my dad. What about you? Why is Amelia Perkins, gorgeous, senior lecturer at a university still single?"

"Because I am waiting for someone who gets me." Amelia smiled sadly. "It's amazing how important that is to me."

Travis nodded. "Yes, I would imagine so."

And then he couldn't help himself. "Do you know a business student in your department, Skyler Porter?"

Amelia seemed put out by the change of subject, but she nodded.

"Yes, I do know her. I taught her Macro Economics."

"What type of student was she?" Travis leaned forward, his interest more than piqued now.

"She was good. Sharp as a tack." Amelia smiled. "She is brilliant. Why, is she a friend's daughter or something?"

"She is a friend of the family," Travis said vaguely. "It's something she doesn't talk about. So I wouldn't tell her that you know. She thinks we are highly uncool."

"Wow," Amelia widened her eyes. "Who would have thought it? She is so unassuming. I have never heard her namedrop, not once."

"That's her." Travis changed the subject. If he wasn't careful, he would inquire about Sky all night. He didn't want the conversation to devolve into that.

His earlier ruminations about Sky had his brain buzzing with thoughts of her. He felt like driving up to Mount Faith and getting their first meeting over with.

He would look her in the eye, feel nothing and then his twenty-one-year obsession would be over.

Or he could channel his thoughts elsewhere. Amelia was looking at him with open adoration, and he liked it. He more than liked it.

"So what are you doing this weekend?" he found himself asking, "I have a boat..."

Chapter Twenty

May 1998

"How is it possible that you are graduating university already?" Emma moaned to Sky. "You just got here."

"I got here three years ago, and I did two years of summer," Sky smiled happily. "When you think about it, if you work flat out to finish your degree, it is doable."

Sky was in the University records office waiting to get her graduation package and make sure that her grades were all in their database and accounted for.

Emma had followed her, hoping to share her woes about her grades. As usual, her headphone was around her neck.

"My parents said I had to work this summer." Emma grimaced. "What are you doing?"

"Harvard tour." Sky chuckled. "My MBA begins in August. It's gonna be fun."

"I am a tiny bit envious." Emma shrugged. "Maybe this

year I'll get serious."

Sky smirked. "Yes, I've heard this before."

She was about to add something else when Amelia Perkins walked into the office. As usual, she was dressed impeccably and looked like she was strutting on a runway somewhere instead of being an educator. She spotted Sky in the crowded waiting room and stopped.

"Skyler!" She said it like they were long lost friends.

"Hello, Miss Perkins." Sky waved to her.

She walked over to Sky and smiled. "Let us do lunch, today."

"Me?" Sky stuttered, she glanced at Emma in shock and then back at Amelia.

"Of course you, silly," Amelia laughed. "Where have you been hiding out, I haven't seen you on campus since last year."

"I, er don't live on campus," Sky said hoping that her incredulity wasn't showing. She had never spoken to Amelia Perkins outside of class in her three years of being at Mount Faith.

"Oh, that's right." Amelia nodded. "There is so much I don't know about you."

Emma was widening her eyes and looking slack-jawed between Sky and Amelia.

"Well see you at one," Amelia said smiling. "Faculty dining room. I heard they have lasagna on the menu today, yum."

She walked away her hips swaying.

"What just happened?" Emma asked looking at Sky. "When since you and Amelia Perkins started having lunch together?"

Sky looked at Emma in bewilderment. "I have no idea what just happened myself."

****

The faculty dining room was near empty when Sky showed up at five minutes to one. She was more curious than ever about her meeting with Amelia.

She had no clue what it could be about.

She looked around, and Amelia wasn't there. She recognized a few of her past lecturers. She was not really into socializing with them. It would be awkward. She was just about to turn and leave when Amelia showed up.

"Hey Sky," Amelia was grinning at Sky like they were long lost, friends.

"Hello again Miss Perkins," Sky said apprehensively. Why was she getting all of this attention from this lecturer?

"Ah, call me Amelia. Let's head for the food line, and then we'll talk."

They chose their dishes. Amelia insisted on paying for Sky's food and then they sat in the back of the cafeteria.

"Away from prying eyes and listening ears," Amelia said conspiratorially.

"What's this about?" Sky asked before she took a bite of her food. "Are you changing my grade for the Econ course or..."

"Oh none of that," Amelia fanned her questions off. "This is personal."

Amelia inhaled. "My er significant other said you were a friend of his family and that I shouldn't mention him to you. I tried to keep my distance, but it is so hard. You are leaving this semester, and I wanted to pick your brain about him and the family a bit."

"Oh," Sky chuckled too relieved to even pay attention to what Amelia was saying, "I thought it had to do with my grades!"

"No, no." Amelia smiled. "You can relax about that. I hear your A's are so straight that they have to use a ruler to line them up."

Sky grinned. "That is so; I have a perfect GPA. So who is your fiancé?"

"I won't say his name." Amelia grinned, "I did promise him on more than one occasion to not mention him to you."

"Intriguing." Sky laughed, "so how can I tell you anything about him if I don't know who we are talking about?"

Amelia grinned. "We'll get by, I want to be able to say honestly if it ever came up that I never once mentioned him to you."

"Ah," Sky nodded, "clever."

"So," Amelia took a bite of her lasagna and made a face. "Too heavy and bland."

Sky looked down at the big slice she took for herself and grimaced. "I wasn't that hungry anyway."

Amelia put her fork down. "I want to get married, and he's a commitment-phobe. I have never seen anything like it. He literally shies away from the very word commitment. If I say engagement, he looks like he is about to faint. Marriage, he gets apoplectic.

"We've been seeing each other seriously for a year now, and he has never invited me to stay over at his apartment. He has never introduced me to his family. I mean, it's crazy. My brother spends more time with my boyfriend than I do."

Sky made a face. "That can't be good."

"I mean he is fabulous," Amelia said wistfully. "He is tall dark handsome rich considerate, romantic but unavailable. It's like when I am with him there is somebody else there between us like I do not have his full attention."

Sky was intrigued. Amelia had never spoken to her before,

and now she was pouring out her relationship problems on her like she was a part of her inner circle.

"I know you know who I am talking about," Amelia winked at her. "I know you are close to the family. I visited his apartment once, and there were portraits of you in the living room, and passageway from you were very young to now."

Sky shook her head. "I still have no clue who you are talking about. Just tell me. I'll not say a word."

"Ah come on, Sky," Amelia said frowning. "His brother said you are dear to their hearts. He is the only family member I have met so far and only because we were at dinner and it was unavoidable. He keeps me away from his precious family like I was too common for them or something. It is frustrating! I am too fine to be a deep dark secret. Even for him."

"Then leave," Sky said. *Who on earth could Amelia be talking about? Was it the Wallace's, Addi's mother's side of the family? Would they have pictures of her around or her mother's side of the family? She had dutifully sent her graduation pictures to most of them. And her mother had sent pictures in the past.*

"Are you crazy?" Amelia looked at Sky almost cross-eyed. "You know I can't fathom you if I was that close to such an influential family I would not be so secretive about it. And I am not going to leave the most eligible bachelor on the planet for anything. I just need a shoe in. I need him to love me, to fall crazily and completely in love with me."

"Do you love him?" Sky asked gently. Amelia was acting much unlike the totally together lecturer she had seen leading her class.

"Of course I love him." Amelia groaned. "I love him so much sometimes it hurts."

"I am sorry Amelia," Sky sighed, "I can't help. You can't make people love you. I still have no idea who..."

"Just tell me if there is someone else." Amelia interrupted her impatiently, "Tell me if there is something I can do to get him to focus all his attention on me."

Sky sighed. "This is what I would tell my girlfriends if they asked me the same thing. Give him an ultimatum; if he loves you even a little bit, he won't want to lose you. Are you sure that it was my pictures you saw?"

"Yes." Amelia was staring off into space.

"But how..." Sky didn't get to finish her sentence.

Amelia got up. "Thank you, Sky. You just gave me a brilliant idea. We'll chat some more later."

Then she was gone, hurrying through the dining room like she had something urgent to do.

Sky stared at the chunk of lasagna and got up too.

The video for The Boy Is Mine was playing on the lone television in the now empty dining room.

She stopped and listened to it in its entirety. It was going to be her new jam for 1998 even though she had no boy to claim.

Chapter Twenty-One

"**A**re all your needs being met, Mr. Jefferson?" The question was business related. Travis looked at the asker, Jasper Lewin, was a shrewd negotiator who wanted to extend his current relationship with Jefferson Pharmaceuticals.

He nodded and pointed to the contract. "Everything seems okay. Your company has been outstanding so far."

They shook hands, and he walked with Jasper to the door and told Betty to hold his calls. He was feeling as glum as the weather outside. It had been raining for most of May, mostly in the evenings but he was probably the only one in the entire country who was feeling so constricted in his head.

The country was hyped up about the FIFA world cup in France. It was the first time that the Jamaican Reggae Boys were representing on the world stage and everyone including his father, a staunch golf lover, was suddenly a football fan.

But here he was dissatisfied, unfulfilled. He was missing something. His emotional needs were not being met.

He glanced at the calendar on his desk; he had circled blue around the date July 11— Sky's graduation.

He had to wait two more years while she completed her masters.

He sighed.

He was getting tired of waiting, and he didn't have to. He could just start a relationship with her now, get this anticipation over with. He needed to meet her. The longer he waited, the more the anticipation was devouring his life.

His phone rang. He picked it up; it had to be important. He had told Betty to hold his calls.

"Travis," Betty cleared her throat, "there is a lady out here who's claiming to be your girlfriend. She is demanding to see you."

"Amelia?" Travis asked.

"Yes that's her name," Betty said in relief. "Should I send her in?"

"Yes." Travis closed his eyes and then turned around when the door opened. He was casually sitting at the edge of his desk, and he didn't crack a smile when he saw Amelia's anxious face.

He wasn't amused. This was the first time she was intruding on his business space. They usually went to dinner and his suite at the Jamaica Pegasus. He liked to keep her out of what he considered his main life. Amelia was just his lover with hardly any emotional ties to go with it.

He liked it like that. Amelia said she understood that that was how it had to be.

"Hi," She smiled at him tentatively.

"Hi." Travis folded his arms. No greeting in his tone.

"This is a nice office." She spun around and looked at the plants and then the view of the mountains.

"Sorry to drop by so unexpectedly but I have unexpected,

exciting news!"

Travis raised an eyebrow, no humor in his face. "What is it?"

"I am pregnant!" Amelia walked up to him and kissed him on the lips.

Travis recoiled in shock. "What?"

"P.R.E.G.N.A.N.T." She spelled out the letters in between little kisses on his cheek. "I am carrying the next Jefferson heir."

Travis froze. Literally. He never imagined that hearing this kind of news would make him feel so genuinely devastated. Maybe, because it was coming from the wrong woman. This wasn't how it was meant to be.

"You do not look pleased." Amelia pulled away from him.

"This is a lot to take in." Travis focused on her and then looked away. "And it is a little odd your phrasing, 'you are carrying the next Jefferson heir.' We are not the royal family you know?"

Amelia cupped her belly protectively and avoided answering him. "Why are you like this, so cold? "

"I am not cold. Just shocked." Travis moved away from his desk and went to the patio and looked out.

"If we get married in a few weeks we can pretend that this isn't a shotgun marriage," Amelia said helpfully. "I know that you are the CEO of a large company and having a child out of wedlock is not your cup of tea."

Travis nodded, it wasn't. Appearances were important in his line of work. Besides, his dream was to have children with one woman, his wife.

Marriage. He hadn't even thought about that possibility with Amelia, and he had used protection every time, and she had claimed to be on the pill.

"I think I should meet your parents." Amelia sat down in

one of the guest chairs and crossed her legs. "I am booked in at the Pegasus for the rest of the week."

"Give me some time to think," Travis said sharper than he had intended. He heard Amelia gasp.

"I'll call you." He looked over his shoulder at her and tried to smile to soften the blow. "Maybe we can have a private dinner later in the suite."

He waited until he heard her leave the room and the door click in place before he slumped his shoulders in defeat. He had messed this up.

****

Duke's apartment was across from his at the Jefferson Building. Travis had just had a tension-filled dinner with Amelia where he had sat down and listened incredulously as she outlined their wedding. Which designer she was going to use for her dress, the location, their honeymoon.

"It has to be huge." She had grinned like a Cheshire cat. "As your wife who do you think I should align myself with?"

Amelia had asked with a dreamy look in her eyes. "The art crowd, the business crowd or should I position myself as a charity maven? You know, continue with your disabled charity efforts. Why disabilities though? Why not animals, that's more my cup of tea."

Travis had not reacted.

"Come on, Travis," she had rubbed her belly. "We need to plan this."

It was no wonder that he was walking in the rain all the way to the Jefferson Building. He had left his car in the parking lot because he needed to think.

Throughout dinner, the one question that he kept on asking himself was, what was Amelia like in the timeline before?

Had he met her?

He had not recorded a thing about her anywhere. Not one line. And he had a feeling after listening to her at dinner that this whole scenario was wrong.

He walked straight to his shower when he went into the apartment he was dripping wet anyway.

He allowed the water to sluice all over his face and hair and he searched his brain for a solution to this dilemma that he was now facing.

There was nothing. He was going to have to marry this woman who he currently had no feelings for, who seemed to be an unashamed social climber. She was planning their wedding, and he hadn't even proposed.

The rest of his life was going to be hell. In the previous timeline he was imprisoned in a wheelchair, this time he would be imprisoned in a marriage.

And what about Sky?

The thought came to him when he was getting dressed. She had loved him when he was Travis Jefferson, a crippled university lecturer.

He passed her pictures on his way out the apartment, stopping to stare at her graduation picture where she was in cap and gown, a smile on her pretty face. Garfield had acquired her pre-graduation photos for him. He had it framed.

He imagined her eyes accusing him of being an idiot. He opened the door to his apartment and saw his father in the corridor standing before Duke's apartment a six-pack of beer in his hands.

"He told you about the new big screen television?" Travis asked grinning.

"Yup." Miguel grinned and then squinted at him. "What's wrong?"

"I'll come and tell you." Travis closed his door at the same time Duke opened his.

"I am coming over," Travis looked up.

Duke nodded. "Cool. I don't drink, Dad," he muttered gesturing to the beer.

"This is Milly's veggie beer," Miguel snorted. "You had better have this, there is more at home, much more."

Travis headed to the apartment and was promptly handed a veggie beer, which surprisingly didn't taste bad.

"Milly could make a go of producing this." He held it up to the light. It was green.

"Uh-huh," Miguel mumbled. "It shouldn't be called beer. Maybe veggie soda?"

Duke still had not touched his. "I refuse to taste it."

"Come on, support your sister," Miguel laughed, "rescue me from the loads of the stuff she dumped at the house."

Travis watched the day's football match with his dad and Duke and then he told them the news.

"Are you sure she's pregnant?" Duke was the one to ask after Travis finished telling them his story.

Miguel turned down the volume on the television and looked at him.

"I don't know." Travis sighed. "She is already planning our wedding and is talking about being the mother of the Jefferson heir."

"Jefferson heir?" Duke whispered, and then he laughed. "Are we royalty?"

"That's the same thing I asked," Travis smirked. "Maybe she thought the name Duke was a title."

"I knew she was a social climber the minute I spotted her at dinner with you that night," Duke said. "Don't marry her. You'll regret it."

Miguel sighed. "But on the other hand, if she's pregnant with your child it is the responsible thing to do. Bring her to the house to meet us. Your mother won't care if she is the witch of Endor if she is carrying her grandchild."

"What about Sky?" Duke asked. "Your other timeline girl. The woman you have been talking about for the last twenty odd years, long before she was even born? What about her?"

"I don't know." Travis got up and stretched.

"I think you should contact her," Duke said, "Write her emails anonymously and when she is done with school, get her a job here at Jefferson's. You'll get to see her every day. You guys will fall in love again, and you'll live happily ever after. Music— the end."

"Good idea." Miguel nodded, "but there is still the pregnant girl. What's her name?"

"Amelia Perkins," Travis answered absently. He was already thinking of Duke's idea. *Contact with Sky.*

He could easily get her email address from Garfield. The next two years wouldn't be so lonely after all.

"Thanks, guys," he nodded to Duke. "I think you are the best brother in the world, you know that?"

"Of course I am," Duke said. "I want you to be happy. You have been sad for a while because of your crazy self-imposed no contact with Skyler Porter. This Amelia girl won't make you happy."

Chapter Twenty-Two

Summer 1999

Sky had the AC blasting on high in Josh's, Upper East Side Apartment in Manhattan. It was the hottest summer in New York's history. She was sure of it even if the news channels weren't constantly saying so. The heat was like a living thing a wall of impenetrable resistance. She was happy that she had opted to do an Internet-based business for her compulsory internship for the summer.

This way she got to stay inside. She got to create her own company from scratch, and she got to hang with Addi who had a cushy job as a model for the summer, and she got to spend as much time with her Internet buddy, her unhealthy obsession, TJ.

They had started corresponding in the summer of '98. He said he was lonely and he was a secret admirer who had been watching her at Mount Faith.

She had found it funny at the time and a little suspicious, but he could tell her specific things about herself.

They had quickly moved on from their initial communication to long letters multiple times per day, and she should admit she was addicted. He was like a sounding board.

"He may just be a she," Addi intoned behind her. "You have fallen in love with a girl."

"Shut up!" Sky looked up from her new laptop. "Why are you hanging around in my head? Shouldn't you be off somewhere having your Barbie doll face painted, showing off your ridiculously long hair and posing prettily?"

"You sound envious." Addi opened the fridge and then grimaced. "We need groceries."

"The buffet at the hotel around the corner is low priced," Sky muttered. "If I lived here I would never cook. Hence no need for groceries."

Addi grabbed a bottle of water and shook her head, "that buffet has too many things I just have to sample. If I gain a pound the camera will pick it up."

"Don't be crazy, just say no to cake on weekdays, yes on weekends." Sky looked at Addi. "You are turning into one of those fussy model women."

"Only for the summer." Addi shook her head. "Do you understand how much money I make at one photo shoot? It's crazy! I shouldn't have gone to school. I should have done this and then save and then do something with the money."

"Hey, watch it." Sky frowned at her. "After this letter to TJ, I have to work on my online business… I don't want to hear stuff like that, education is important.

"Repeat after me, labor for learning before you grow old for learning is better than silver and gold, silver and gold will vanish away, but a good education will never decay."

Addi grinned. "Unless you get hit over the head, and you

forget all you've labored to learn."

The phone rang. Addi answered and then squealed. "Here? Now? Okay."

"What?" Sky frowned.

"Josh is bringing home a friend." Addi leaned on the wall.

"Okay." Sky nodded. "Is the friend female. Are we going to have to hide in the room while he entertains?"

"No." Addi twirled her waist-length curls around her fingers. "Remember Randy?"

"Yes." Sky grinned, "Chocolate Randy, Hunk on legs. I do remember him."

"Well, they met at a technology conference in the city." He told Randy we were here and Randy said he wanted to see us again."

"Cool!" Sky nodded. "It would be good to see how much hunkier he has become. He was pretty spectacular eight years ago."

Addi groaned. "I am single. I have no life. I still live with my brother. He is going to think I am pathetic!"

"You are gorgeous, and modeling and just finished your first degree. You live in the Upper East Side in an apartment with a view. Didn't you have a boyfriend last month?"

"Neville." Addi sighed. "He doesn't count. We weren't serious."

"I should tell TJ that your lover from another time is coming over."

"Don't mention my name to your secret internet friend," Addi warned. "You don't know who this guy or girl is!"

Sky snorted. "Even if I tell him he wouldn't believe me. Relax. Tell me who on this earth would take the whole resetting phenomena seriously?"

"I am going to change." Addi ran to the room that they shared. Sky rolled her eyes. She was in a slip dress, cotton with little yellow flowers on it. She had no desire to change into anything else. Besides, she was not interested in Randy.

She was interested in no one.

Well, except TJ, though she didn't know who he was.

Well, she knew, sort of. He ran a business, a family business. He generally told her about his day. He attended a lot of meetings.

She figured he couldn't be too busy because he always wrote her back as soon as she wrote to him.

One night or was it early morning she had terrible period cramps, and she had written him at two in the morning. He had written her back. He had stayed up with her and distracted her from the pain.

She wrote him now. She glanced at the clock. It was just eleven forty-five.

My cousin Addi's lover from another time is coming to visit. She is panicking. She hasn't seen him since 1992... when she changed the timeline. She put a smiley face after the sentence and waited.

TJ would probably laugh at her, ask her which movie she was watching.

She waited for his response and got none. Josh even came by with Randy by then she had stopped checking.

Randy looked delicious. Even Sky had to admit that. He was the type of guy whose biceps women would squeeze to see if they were real, and he had the kind of face that made you look twice and then wonder what kind of genetic mixture made him stand out so much.

He even made Josh look ordinary, and Josh was good-looking.

They chitchatted for a while.

Randy was anxious to see Addi. Sky could tell he kept looking at the door of the bedroom.

"Isn't she coming out?" Randy asked Sky again.

Sky grinned. "I have no clue."

But just then Addi came out of the bedroom in the same outfit she had run in with initially—cut off jeans shirt and singlet top with curls streaming down her back and a face devoid of makeup.

"Hello Randy," she said solemnly.

Randy didn't respond for a while. It was crazy; Sky actually thought he was speechless.

Addi made Randy speechless.

She heard a ping, which indicated to her that she had new mail and she opened her laptop quickly. It was TJ!

Was in a meeting.

How did the meeting go? Sky wrote back: *Are you seriously not going to laugh at me?*

TJ wrote: *No. Why would I?*

Because I said time travel and timeline and all of that fictional stuff.

TJ wrote: *I haven't seen you since 1975 when I changed my timeline. So I guess I won't laugh.*

Sky laughed out loud and typed back. *I knew you weren't serious. I was born 1977.*

Josh looked over at her. "What's so funny?"

"Just talking with my friend."

Josh sighed. "I see I am like an extra wheel here. Anybody want us to go to lunch?"

Sky looked across at Randy and Addi; they were talking, more with their eyes than their lips. They were like magnets to each other. The rest of the room was forgotten.

"I'll pass." Sky snorted and looked back down at her computer.

"Me too," Josh muttered. "Hey buddy, Randy! I am going back to the conference."

"Sure," Randy said not shifting from his seat. His eyes fixed firmly on Addi.

****

December 31, 1999

I want to meet you before the world ends.

Travis was sitting on the patio at his parent's house. He had the laptop on the table. He was instant messaging Sky. They had graduated from email for a couple of months now.

He looked at the simple line, and he almost gave in.

She was in Boston, hadn't bothered to fly home for the Christmas. Her family had met up in New York.

Josh had bought a house in Manhattan, and they had a party there. She had just flown home to Boston.

He knew more about Sky and what she was thinking and doing than he had ever hoped for. They were having a long distance relationship without explicitly stating that it was what they were having.

He typed back quickly: *Why meet now?*

She hated when he took long to respond.

Because everything will go boom at 12. She typed back. *The world will stop.*

He typed: *But Addi said that she experienced the year 2017, obviously, there won't be a boom tonight.*

He chuckled when he was typing that.

Sky typed back: *I still can't get over the fact that you believe me about resetters. Why do I want to meet you now? Because I just want to ... I want to put a face to the repository of my thoughts for the last year and a half.*

He replied with the thought that was paramount on his

mind: *I want to hug you, pull you close to me never let go.*

She was silent for a long time. He had never written her anything so explicit and overly intimate.

They shared everything over the past couple of months, the inane and the exciting, and yet he hadn't ever stepped over the line until now.

When can we finally meet? She responded to him.

Travis sighed in relief. *When you are done with school. I am here in Jamaica waiting.*

Are you sure that after all this time you are not a girl?

Travis laughed and then wrote. *I am sure. And all my parts seem to be in working order.*

Sky typed: *Do you have any secrets I should know about?*

He was about to write, and then he pulled back his hands from the keyboard.

"Honey," his mother came to the patio entrance. "Come and join us inside for the countdown."

"Coming." Travis looked up and smiled at her. "Let me just finish this conversation."

His mother looked at the computer and then at him. "You people and those things."

He wrote to Sky: *I have secrets and I will share them with you face to face. Goodnight and Happy New Year. You are the loveliest girl I know.*

****

May 14, 2000

Sky: What does TJ stand for?

You are just asking me this? Travis asked he was on the way from Toronto Airport after a conference.

Sky: Are you cute?

TJ: No. Cats are cute.

Sky: Lol. I got an invitation to an interview in Jamaica. I will be there in a week. My dad is so excited.

As am I. Travis wrote her back, *we should arrange for a place to meet when you get here.*

Sky: Yes. Somewhere where I can run and hide if you turn out to be a monster. Addi still thinks you are a girl or a kook and that I will be disappointed.

TJ: Where is your interview, again?

Sky: Jefferson Pharmaceuticals.

Travis smiled when he saw that response and wrote back: *That's quite a scoop just after leaving college.*

Yes, it is. Sky wrote. *They are huge.*

TJ: I hope we'll have time to meet up after your interview. Have lunch. The Pegasus.

Chapter Twenty-Three

Summer 2000

"I am sorry Miss Porter, but you are not qualified for this job," Mrs. Beckett held out her hand to be shaken.

She didn't look sorry. Sky looked at her outstretched arm and considered for just a split second to be rude, but she didn't. She shook the lady's hand and searched for something to say that was pleasant, something that didn't scream her disappointment.

The door to the office was unceremoniously opened before she could formulate a word and a rather handsome guy pushed his head around the door.

"Oh good, she is here. Send her to my office Bertha, will you?"

Sky frowned and looked from Mrs. Beckett to the mysterious gentleman.

Mrs. Beckett looked miffed. "But I already checked over

her résumé as you asked me to do, sir, and I think..."

He came fully into the room. He was tall, over six feet. He had dark nutmeg brown skin and jet-black wavy hair, which was brushing his collar—some of it was falling in his chocolate brown eyes. He was the definition of tall, dark and handsome.

He pushed his hand into his suit pocket and looked at Sky for longer than was polite and then back at Mrs. Beckett.

"This interview was supposed to be a formality, Bertha. If I didn't have that meeting, I would have been around to welcome Sky into the Jefferson Pharmaceutical family."

And then his magnetic brown eyes were eating her up. "I am sorry for the misunderstanding, Skyler." He moved from the doorway and advanced to her a smile in his eyes.

"My name is Travis Jefferson. Will you be so kind as to walk with me to my office?"

Sky nodded as if she was in a daze. He called her Sky with a hint of familiarity that was puzzling and exciting at the same time.

This was the Travis Jefferson, the head of the company. She had no idea he was so young, maybe early thirties and no idea that he was so attractive. Sky tried not to stare when she walked closer to him. She could smell his cologne—something earthy.

She had the insane urge to stop and sniff him. Instead, she concentrated on looking professional and followed him to the bank of elevators.

His office was three floors up from where she met Mrs. Beckett. He stood apart from her in the elevator and stared at her as if he wanted to say something. Sky felt a little bit self-conscious. She suffered through his silent regard and then followed him through the carpeted hallway and into his office.

Up here in the hallowed hallways of richness was obviously where the executives resided. Every door had a name embossed in brass, each of which had a VP of whatever on it.

His door was wider than the rest. The office was large and tastefully done. There was a stonewall with little flowerpots filled with live plants at one corner. It had a small conference table at one end and his desk in the middle. There was a patio filled with plants and a view of the mountains in the distance.

"Nice." Sky looked around.

Travis indicated for her to sit in a seat across from him and then he leaned over the desk smiling. "I have been keeping track of your educational pursuits, Miss Porter."

"You have?" Sky was trying not to act surprised.

But he could see that she was. He scratched his head and then laughed. "My God, it is going to take time explaining this to you."

"What are you going on about?" Sky asked frowning. "Do you know me from somewhere?"

He smiled. "I believe I do Miss Porter. Not from some other place but some other time."

"Some other time?" Sky raised an eyebrow.

"I am ridiculously pleased to meet you in person." Travis continued. He could hardly believe that she was here. He had waited for her for over twenty years. He would never wish this kind of wait on anyone.

"We should have lunch together. Talk a bit." Travis suggested gently. He was trying so hard not to stare but good lord she was the most beautiful woman in the world to him.

"Oh," Sky opened her mouth in awe, "Well I er, I sort of have a lunch appointment with er..." She swallowed. "Of course Mr. Jefferson we can er have lunch."

"That is the last time you call me Mr. Jefferson," Travis grinned at her, "I am just plain old Travis or TJ but only in private. I actually dislike the moniker TJ, but for the purposes of getting in touch with you, it had to do."

Sky squealed. "What? No!"

"Yes." Travis laughed at her.

"But..." Sky swallowed, "but TJ went to Mount Faith. He knew things about me!"

"As did I. I went to Mount Faith in the other timeline. You were my student, and I was your teacher. I was in a wheelchair, and we fell in love.

"You were the one who told me about resetters. I had that 't' in my palms. You took a bullet for me. I was so grief-stricken I went back to reset things. 1975 was the year to do it because I wanted to save my brother from being a murderer.

"I met Gwen Fisher Campbell, the very day after she wrote her diary and your stepmother Monica. I wonder if she will recognize me now?"

Sky was looking at Travis transfixed. "I...what."

"Go slower?" Travis asked gently.

"Yes." Sky nodded.

"Well, it's a good thing I arranged to take the rest of the week off." Travis stood up, "let's go."

****

They had lunch at Travis' apartment, which was a revelation to Sky. Her pictures were everywhere.

"You are the friend that Amelia was going on about?" Sky asked as she walked slowly through the passageway. "How did you get my graduation picture? How did you know I had this dress?"

She moved on to another picture and gawped at them.

"Garfield gave me your grad picture and that gray dress was something you wore in the other timeline."

"My creepy next door neighbor?" Sky grimaced, "that guy was always watching me."

"Sorry, my fault," Travis murmured.

They headed back to the living room. Sky was feeling a little bit overwhelmed. This was her TJ? This gorgeous guy? She told him everything. The Internet had made her a bit more liberal than she would have been otherwise in a relationship. She reflected on all the things that they had shared.

She looked away from Travis in embarrassment. The time travel bit was an extra dimension she couldn't even handle right now

Travis walked closer to her and stood in front of her. "I told you everything too. Well, most things."

Sky groaned. "This is hard."

"No." Travis smiled. "This is exactly how it should be."

"So what happened with Amelia?" Sky asked belatedly. She had forgotten about Amelia's bizarre lunch conversation two years ago. "Are you married to her?"

Travis smiled. "How would that make you feel?"

"Like crap." Sky's voice trembled, "betrayed, I fell in love with TJ. I mean, you. You could have told me that you were married."

"I love you too, Sky. It feels as if I have for a very, very long time." Travis got up and walked to her side of the settee and pulled her into his arms.

"Are you married to Amelia Perkins?"

"Hell no," Travis whispered in her hair. "The lady confessed to trying to dupe me because I was a commitment-phobe and I needed a gentle push. I broke up with her that very night."

Sky hugged him to her. She didn't know how long they stayed like that.

Travis was the one who finally pulled away and then

cupped her cheek in his. "Sky will you marry me?"

"Yes." Sky blinked. "Shouldn't we spend some time getting used to each other face to face first."

"I guess we could do that. How does a week sound?" Travis asked. "You meet my family, and I meet yours, and then we get married, somewhere, anywhere, I don't care, I just want to make sure that you are mine and then we'll spend the next three or so weeks naked and horizontal. I don't care where just that you are here with me."

Sky leaned in to kiss him. "Sounds like a plan. A very good plan."

The End

Here is an excerpt from
Now or Never

Skyler's Wedding- July 2000

"So we meet again, Addi."

Addi knew it was Randy even before she turned around. She had been aware of him through the whole service and then the reception. In a room full of good-looking men he was a standout. She was sure that she was not the only female who was ogling him.

She turned around slowly from where she was to take him in fully and then just like that her once steady hands started to tremble on the glass of wine.

"Randy didn't see you there." She was trying for nonchalant. She failed.

"Liar." Randy laughed. "It was a nice wedding. You made a beautiful maid of honor."

"Thanks." Addi nodded. "I almost didn't show up. Sky and Travis were crazy enough to plan a large wedding in a mere two weeks."

"But you did come. It's nice to see you again." Randy cleared his throat. "Can we go somewhere quiet and talk?" He looked around the crowded poolside of the Jefferson mansion. "Maybe to the gardens?"

Addi bit her lip and then shook her head. "I don't think so. I meant what I said, Randy. I can't have a relationship with you."

"Yes, I remember," Randy nodded, "Oh I remember last year in New York. You said I was a past mistake and that I had no place in your life this time around."

"That's right." Addi nodded. "I am glad you got the

message."

"I did." Randy shrugged. "I just don't get the reason for the message."

Addi put the drink on a table and then turned around again. "Okay, come on."

Randy raised an eyebrow but did not argue. He followed her as she headed down a cobbled stone walkway all the way to a mini bridge where there was a pond and an unoccupied gazebo.

It was quite picturesque. There were koi in the pond—little colorful bodies glinting in the six o'clock sunlight. Addi stood in the gazebo her hands braced on the railing, her long curly hair in a half up half down hairdo. Her filmy long pink dress floated around her. She looked like a princess waiting for her loyal subject.

"Can I take your picture?" He asked taking out his camera. "This is too lovely a moment not to capture."

Addi seemed like she thought about it for a moment and then she nodded. "Go ahead."

He snapped several shots of her and then smiled. "I guess you are used to this and all, you being a model."

"That was last year." Addi sat in one of the chairs in the gazebo. "This year I am writing a novel."

"That's quite a departure from what you said you were doing before." Randy stepped up into the gazebo and sat before her.

He loosened his bow tie and raised an eyebrow. "In the previous time, you were a doctor in sociology. You should be pursuing a masters degree by now."

"You remembered that?" Addi asked flippantly.

"I remember everything you ever told me." Randy leaned forward and frowned. "I invested in those tech stocks you told me about."

"Good for you." Addi smiled at him, the first genuine smile he was seeing from her in a while.

"I invested some of my money in real estate. After the 96 meltdown, several places were going for cheap."

"And where are you working now, or are you just investing? Addi asked him.

Interest. Finally.

Randy relaxed somewhat. "I am working at Gordon and Fletcher, chief accounting officer for their telecommunications company. That's the reason I was at the tech summit last year in New York."

"That sounds great." Addi looked at him and then away. "Really great."

"I am still not married to any pastor's daughter or have any hopes of joining the ministry." Randy reminded her of what she had told him that he had ended up doing before she had reset things.

"I am very much interested in knowing why we can't be together. You have written me off based on previous information from a timeline that I am not privy to."

Addi sighed. "I don't remember much of what happened. I have this book where I wrote down stuff, and I cautioned myself never to get involved with you."

Randy leaned back in the chair and rubbed the back of his neck. "This is frustrating Addison. You and I have chemistry. It is stupid for us not to explore that in the here and now. I am single. You are single. I have liked you since you were a kid. Now you are a grown, gorgeous woman. You have to give us a chance."

"No!" Addi stood up. "I have other plans."

"You have a boyfriend?" Randy asked belatedly.

"Yes." Addison nodded. "The timing for us is just off."

"I'd say." Randy huffed. "I don't know why I assumed

you were single. Josh never mentioned to me that you were dating."

He got up and stood beside her, looking down in the fishpond. "I guess we aren't meant to be after all."

"I guess so." Addi looked at him, and her lips had a slight tremor. "I am going back to the party."

"You can break it off with him," Randy said holding her hand. "I'll wait."

Addi looked down at their joined hands and then up at Randy. The pulse in her palm was racing, and she knew her voice would be breathless. "I don't think I should."

"You should." Randy leaned toward her so close she could feel the heat from his face. She could feel his breath on her skin. "When you do, call me."

Addi inhaled tremulously and then stepped away from him. "I don't think so. Goodbye Randy."

"Never goodbye," Randy gave her a bitter half-smile, "not between you and me. I have a feeling we were meant to be together..."

OTHER BOOKS BY BRENDA BARRETT

Wiley Brothers Series

Between Brothers (Book 0)- The beginning of the Wiley brothers saga, Joseph Wiley's unconventional family life may prove to be fatal to some members of the family.

For Pete's Sake (Book 1)- Preston has a run in with a child named Pete who claims that he is the grandson of their former housekeeper Pamela Stone.

Crossing Jordan (Book 2)- Jordan is miffed when Shawn takes her new fiancé to Jamaica and insists that he be best man at their wedding.

Fire and Walter (Book 3)- Walter's shady past is affecting his new appointment as church elder. The situation would not only compromise him but a particular newly married church sister as well.

The Perfect Guy (Book 4) - Guy decides to explore the world of farming, becomes an apprentice to a farmer and lives a humble life. He is constantly rebuffed by the woman that he loves because she thinks he is poor!

The Patience of A Saint (Book 5)- Saint attends his own divorce party put on by his soon to be ex wife and they end up complicating matters.

A Case of Love (Book 6)- Case unwittingly buys a bride

from a human trafficking ring a few days before his own wedding.

Resetter Series

Never Too Late (Book 1)- Addi finds out she is a resetter and goes back to the summer of 92 to change her family's lives.

Never Say Never (Book 2)- Skyler's handsome college lecturer, who happens to be her neighbor, has a 't' in his palms. Should she tell him the significance of it. If she does, would he believe her?

Now or Never (Book 3)- Ten years later Addi and Randy meet again at Randy's engagement party. Why is it that the chemistry between them was still so potent? Can they ever have a future together? Would Randy choose her this time around?

Almost Never (Book 4)- Tech genius Joshua Porter had all but given up on love. He then meets Portia, an inmate at the female penitentiary and his life takes a turn for the adventurous.

The Scarlett Family Series

Scarlett Baby (Book 1)- When the head of the Scarlett family died, Yuri had to return home to Treasure Beach for the funeral. What he didn't count on was seeing Marla, his childhood sweetheart and his best friend's wife. And when emotions overwhelm them and a few months later Marla is pregnant, Yuri wants the impossible: his best friend's wife and the baby they made together...

Scarlett Sinner (Book 2)- Pastor Troy Scarlett realizes the hard way that some sins are bound to be revealed, like the child that he had out of wedlock with his wife's mortal enemy from college. His wife Chelsea was not happy with the status quo. She was not taking care of the son of the woman she had so despised from college. And she could not get over the deep betrayal that she felt from her husband's indiscretion.

Scarlett Secret (Book 3)- Terri Scarlett had a soft spot for her friend, Lola. She was funny and sweet and they looked remarkably alike. But when Lola's Arab prince demands his bride, Terri foolishly exchange places with her friend and they meet up on a world of trouble.

Scarlett Love (Book 4)- Slater always looked forward to delivering packages to the law firm where he could get a glimpse of the stunning female lawyer, Amoy Gardener. Unfortunately, for Slater a woman like Amoy would not take him seriously, especially when she found out that he could not read!

Scarlett Promise (Book 5)- Driven by desperation Lisa Barclay decides to make some extra money by prostituting herself after being kicked out in the streets. Her first customer turns out to be a popular government senator and then to her horror he dies...

Scarlett Bride (Book 6)- When Oliver Scarlett's missionary work in the Congo region was coming to an end, he had a decision to make, marry Ashaki Azanga and save her from being the fourth wife to the chief of the village or leave her to her fate and get on with his life...

Scarlett Heart (Book 7)- After receiving a heart transplant shy librarian Noah Scarlett started to take on character traits that were unlike him and he kept dreaming of a girl named Cassandra Green...

Rebound Series

On The Rebound- For Better or Worse, Brandon vowed to stay with Ashley, but when worse got too much he moved out and met Nadine. For the first time in years he felt happy, but then Ashley remembered her wedding vows...

On The Rebound 2- Ashley reinvented herself and was now a first lady in a country church in Primrose Hill, but her obsessed ex friend Regina showed up and started digging into the lives of the saints at church. Somebody didn't like Regina's digging. Someone had secrets that were shocking enough to kill for...

Magnolia Sisters

Dear Mystery Guy (Book 1)- Della Gold details her life in a journal dedicated to a mystery guy. But when fascination turns into obsession she finds herself wanting to learn even more about him but in her pursuit of the mystery guy she begins to learn more about herself...

Bad Girl Blues (Book 2)- Brigid Manderson wanted to go to med school but for the time being she was an escort working for her mother, an ex-prostitute. When her latest customer offers her the opportunity of a lifetime would she take it? Or would she choose the harder path and uncertain love with a Christian guy?

Her Mistaken Dreams (Book 3)- Caitlin Denvers dream guy had serious issues. He has a dead wife in his past and he was the main suspect in her murder. Did he really do it? Or did Caitlin for the first time have a mistaken dream?

Just Like Yesterday (Book 4)- Hazel Brown lost six months of memory including the summer that she conceived her son, and had no idea who his father could be. Now that she had the means to fight to get him back from the Deckers, she finds out that the handsome Curtis Decker is willing to share her son with her after all.

New Song Series

Going Solo (Book 1)- Carson Bell, had a lovely voice, a heart of gold, and was no slouch in the looks department. So why did Alice abandon him and their daughter? What did she want after ten years of silence?

Duet on Fire (Book 2)- Ian and Ruby had problems trying to conceive a child. If that wasn't enough, her ex-lover the current pastor of their church wants her back...

Tangled Chords (Book 3)- Xavier Bell, the poor, ugly duckling has made it rich and his looks have been incredibly improved too. Farrah Knight, hotel heiress had cruelly rejected him in the past but now she needed help. Could Xavier forgive and forget?

Broken Harmony(Book 4)- Aaron Lee, wanted the top job

in his family company but he had a moral clause to consider just when Alka, his married ex-girlfriend walks back into his life.

A Past Refrain (Book 5)- Jayce had issues with forgetting Haley Greenwald even though he had a new woman in his life. Will he ever be able to shake his love for Haley?

Perfect Melody (Book 6)- Logan Moore had the perfect wife, Melody but his secretary Sabrina was hell bent on breaking up the family. Sabrina wanted Logan whatever the cost and she had a secret about Melody, that could shatter Melody's image to everyone.

The Bancroft Family Series

Homely Girl (Book 0) - April and Taj were opposites in so many ways. He was the cute, athletic boy that everybody wanted to be friends with. She was the overweight, shy, and withdrawn girl. Do April and Taj have a love that can last a lifetime? Or will time and separate paths rip them apart?

Saving Face (Book 1) - Mount Faith University drama begins with a dead president and several suspects including the president in waiting Ryan Bancroft.

Tattered Tiara (Book 2) - Micah Bancroft is targeted by femme fatale Deidra Durkheim. There are also several rape cases to be solved.

Private Dancer (Book 3) Adrian Bancroft was gutted when he returned to Jamaica and found out that his first and only love Cathy Taylor was a stripper and was literally owned by the menacing drug lord, Nanjo Jones.

Goodbye Lonely (Book 4) - Kylie Bancroft was shy and had to resort to going to confidence classes. How could she win the love of Gareth Beecher, her faculty adviser, a man with a jealous ex-wife in his past and a current mystery surrounding a hand found in his garden?

Practice Run (Book 5) - Marcus Bancroft had many reasons to avoid Mount Faith but Deidra Durkheim was not one of them. Unfortunately, on one of his visits he was the victim of a deliberate hit and run.

Sense of Rumor (Book 6) - Arnella Bancroft was the wild, passionate Bancroft, the creative loner who didn't mind living dangerously; but when a terrible thing happened to her at her friend Tracy's party, it changed her. She found that courting rumors can be devastating and that only the truth could set her free.

A Younger Man (Book 7) - Pastor Vanley Bancroft loved Anita Parkinson despite their fifteen-year age gap, but Anita had a secret, one that she could not reveal to Vanley. To tell him would change his feelings toward her, or force him to give up the ministry that he loved so much.

Just To See Her (Book 8) - Jessica Bancroft had the opportunity to meet her fantasy guy Khaled, he was finally coming to Mount Faith but she had feelings for Clay Reid, a guy who had all the qualities she was looking for. Who would she choose and what about the weird fascination Khaled had for Clay?

The Three Rivers Series

Private Sins (Book 1)- Kelly, the first lady at Three Rivers Church was pregnant for the first elder of her church. Could she keep the secret from her husband and pretend that all was well?

Loving Mr. Wright (Book 2)- Erica saw one last opportunity to ditch her single life when Caleb Wright appeared in her town. He was perfect for her, but what was he hiding?

Unholy Matrimony (Book 3) - Phoebe had a problem, she was poor and unhappy. Her solution to marry a rich man was derailed along the way with her feelings for Charles Black, the poor guy next door.

If It Ain't Broke (Book 4)- Chris Donahue wanted a place in his child's life. Pinky Black just wanted his love. She also wanted him to forget his obsession with Kelly and love her. That shouldn't be so hard? Should it?

Contemporary Romance/Drama

After The End--Torn between two lovers. Colleen married her high school sweetheart, Isaiah, hoping that they would live happily ever after but life intruded and Isaiah disappeared at sea. She found work with the rich and handsome, Enrique Lopez, as a housekeeper and realized that she couldn't keep him at arms length...

Love Triangle: Three Sides To The Story- George, the husband, Marie, the wife and Karen-the mistress. They all get to tell their side of the story.

The Preacher And The Prostitute - Prostitution and the clergy don't mix. Tell that to ex-prostitute, Maribel, who finds herself in love with the Pastor at her church. Can an ex-prostitute and a pastor have a future together?

New Beginnings - Inner city girl Geneva was offered an opportunity of a lifetime when she found out that her 'real' father was a very wealthy man. Her decision to live up-town meant that she had to leave Froggie, her 'ghetto don,' behind. She also found herself battling with her stepmother and battling her emotions for Justin, a suave up-towner.

Full Circle- After graduating from university, Diana wanted to return to Jamaica to find her siblings. What she didn't foresee was that she would meet Robert Cassidy and that both their pasts would be intertwined, and that disturbing questions would pop up about their parentage, just when they were getting close.

Historical Fiction/Romance

The Empty Hammock- Workaholic, Ana Mendez, fell asleep in a hammock and woke up in the year 1494. It was the time of the Tainos, a time when life seemed simpler, but Ana knew that all of that was about to change.

The Pull Of Freedom- Even in bondage the people, freshly arrived from Africa, considered themselves free. Led by Nanny and Cudjoe the slaves escaped the Simmonds' plantation and went in different directions to forge their destiny in the new country called Jamaica.

Jamaican Comedy (Material contains Jamaican dialect)

Di Taxi Ride And Other Stories- Di Taxi Ride and Other Stories is a collection of twelve witty and fast paced short stories. Each story tells of a unique slice of Jamaican life.